Bruised

For Matthew and Louisa

First published in Great Britain in 2011
by Hodder Children's Books

1

A Catalogue record for this book is available from the British Library

ISBN 978 1 444 90359 1
IRISH EDITION ISBN 978 1 444 90456 7

Type design and layout: www.hereandnowdesign.com

Typeset by Avon DataSet Ltd, Bidford-on-Avon, Warwickshire

Printed and bound in Great Britain by
CPI Bookmarque Ltd, Croydon, Surrey

The paper and board used in this paperback by Hodder Children's Books are natural recyclable products made from wood grown in sustainable forests. The manufacturing processes conform to the environmental regulations of the country of origin.

Hodder Children's Books
a division of Hachette Children's Books
338 Euston Road, London NW1 3BH
An Hachette UK company

www.hachette.co.uk

Bruised

SIOBHÁN PARKINSON

a division of Hachette Children's Books

kind of boy,

a little scrubbed boy . . .

A prating boy.

The Merchant of Venice Act V, Scene 1

Part ONE

chapter **one**

My grandmother died.

I know this is not what you would call a dramatic opening. It's what *happens* to grandparents. They get old (jeez, they *are* old to start with, or they wouldn't *be* grandparents, would they?); they die. (My grandfather died too, actually, but that's another story.)

Mr O'Connell, who is my Creative Writing teacher, which is to say he's my English teacher, but he is into Creative Writing (capital letters deliberate) – he would say, *Not* intriguing *enough, Jonathan. You need to* hook *your reader.*

But, frankly, I couldn't be bothered with the hooking part. See, I don't think you need to start on the premise that your reader (if you have one) is a *fish*.

There used to be a song about that, Gramma used to sing it, about how uneducated fish are, how they can't write their name or read a book – which may or may not have been put in for the rhyme with *brook*. That's where the illiterate fish in question lives, allegedly. Come to think of it, maybe it was the other way round. Maybe *brook* was put in to rhyme with *book*, I mean, because you would think *river*, wouldn't you, in association with fish, not bloody babbling *brook*, like a feckin' poem.

In any case, I don't need to do any hooking, because this is not Creative Writing. This is what really happened, and if you are reading this you will have your own reasons that have nothing to do with fish.

I could have begun by telling you that my mother was a drunk. Or that my father had left. I could have begun by saying, *My mother brought home a bag of apples one night for dinner.* Sounds kinda cutesy, that.

Except that was *all*. A bag of apples. There was nothing else to eat in the house. Not even a loaf of bread. Not a crumb. And we hadn't had much for lunch either.

"Keeps a doctor away," she said, poking her fingernail in the side of the polythene bag to open it.

Right, yeah, very healthy, apples.

When she'd gouged a big enough hole in the bag, she shook the apples out all over the coffee table. Most of them rolled to the edge and then clunked on to the carpet, where they rolled some more.

“Have you heard about the food pyramid?” I asked, fishing for apples under the sofa.

“Pyr-mid?” she said. She stuck a finger in her ear, to represent thinking. Very amusing. “Egypt, right?”

Then she went off into these howls of laughter.

I knew where that would end, so I got ready for it. And by the time I come back into the living room with the basin from the kitchen sink and a dry tea towel, she’s already got to the sobbing stage. Sure enough, as soon as she sees me, she clutches for the basin and pukes up half a litre of sherry. Not the cooking kind. She prefers Fino, she says, which is supposed to make her not a drunk but a connoisseur.

She’s not a connoisseur. She just knew a Spanish word for a kind of sherry that is not so sweet it’d curl your teeth.

I might as well have started this story with the bag of apples after all, because I’ve got there pretty fast, though I didn’t mean to. I meant to explain about my grandmother. Gramma we called her, because she didn’t like *granny* – made her sound like a granny, she said. That was the kind of humour she had. Dead unfunny. (A small voice in my head wants me to revise that last bit, edit out the insensitive word, but on second thoughts, I don’t think so.) Appreciated only by a select group, she used to say about her sense of humour.

Of one, I said. That made her smirk. Old ladies don't go in for smirking, but Gramma did. She liked a good smirk, did Gram.

She didn't live with us or anything like that. She lived near enough. Near enough to supervise, I mean. She went in for supervision. Supervision and smirking. Makes her sound like the granny from hell, but she wasn't. She was sound.

I did miss her. I missed a good hot dinner that didn't come out of one of those Pot Noodle tubs for a start. I missed my five clean shirts every Sunday night, all ironed and on hangers for school. Yes, I *can* iron my own shirts – I may be sad, but I am not a sad bastard – but only *if* I have remembered to wash them in the first place, and to take them out of the machine before they go manky with mould, and hang them up to dry. And, see, that sequence of events didn't happen many weeks, and never two weeks in a row. So of course I missed my grandmother.

But mostly, I missed someone who knew what to do about Julie. I haven't mentioned her before, because I just don't know what to say. That's the real bitch about all this.

That came out wrong. Julie is not a bitch. She's just a little girl whose grandmother is dead and has no parents to speak of. And if you think it's bad for me – I am fourteen after all, I can find *some* sort of way to get by – it's a whole lot worse for an eight-year-old with a big imagination and a tiny understanding and a great gawping hole where the love should be.

God, I dunno where *that* came out of, a great gawping hole where the love should be. Maybe I could get a job working for a greeting card company, writing the prayery kind of words they have on the insides of cards that have a photograph of a bluebell on the front, or a sunset.

Anyway it was the apples that started it, but it wasn't because of the apples that I rang the police. (I am not that thick.) It was when she hit Julie.

I mean, I couldn't have *that*, could I? She's only a little kid. Well, she's eight, but she's young for eight, if you know what I mean. She's not stupid or anything, she's good at school and all that. It's just that she's . . . well . . . it's as if you could break her if you dropped her. Maybe it's because of the *situation*, or maybe it's just the way she is.

She cried when Ma hit her. She may be young for her age, but she's not a crybaby, and I think it wasn't even so much because it hurt, but because she was just so totally *dazed*. No one ever hit her before. I mean, yeah, a smack on the back of the hand if she's reaching for one biscuit too many or a biff on the shoulder to steer her out of the path of some kind of disaster, but a blow full in the face, a blow so hard I could hear the impact – that is not on. That is *assault*.

So there's Julie sitting on the floor surrounded by apples, all snot coming down her face and her wispy, mousy hair catching in it so parts of it are wet and clumpy, and she's gulping with sobs and letting out this high-pitched wail, and Ma all rolled up tight in an armchair with her legs under her, her head tucked into her chest so you can only see the top of her hair, and her arms over her ears, and rocking, rocking, and me in the middle of it all with the portable phone in my hand, dialling 999.

She must have heard the pips, because she looked up before I even spoke and let out an almighty yell at me.

"Garda," I roared over her yell, into the mouthpiece of the phone. I shouldn't have roared, because that word, at that decibel level, really got to Ma, and she came bounding out of her chair and knocked the phone out of my hand.

"Don't you *dare* call the police!" she snarled, pulling my ears so that I had to lower my face to hers and got the stench of booze and vomit off her breath. "Just don't you dare. You are in my house, you are under my roof, and you do *not* . . ." She couldn't bring herself to name my crime, evidently.

She pushed me in the chest, so I staggered backwards and nearly fell on top of Julie, who was still howling on the floor.

"Hello?" came a squeaky little voice from under the sofa, where the phone lay on its back on the floor. "Hello?" A lifeline.

I picked the phone up, but I didn't grab the lifeline. Instead, I pressed the hang-up button.

If the police came, God knows where it would end.

I know they try to keep families together when they take kids into care, but you can't count on it, can you? And who wants a teenage boy with attitude when they could just have a lovely little smiley girl? But for sure I wasn't going anywhere without Julie.

"Under your roof," I said, "but not under your care, and not under your orders either. From now on, I am in charge in this house. You will bring me your money every week and I will buy the food for us all, and I will cook it and serve it, and you can do the washing and cleaning."

Nah, of course I didn't. (Come on, you didn't really believe that, did you?)

I did press the hang-up button, but I didn't make the speech. I just hauled Julie to her feet and walked her out of the room. She'd stopped wailing by now, but she was still choking on her tears.

I put her up on the kitchen table and washed her face. I clucked over her, and she went on sobbing and sniffing. I tried to dry her face with the kitchen towel, but she said, "Aagh! It stinks," and pushed it away, so I got a tissue and dabbed at her face with that. All along the cheekbone on one side it was swollen, but the skin wasn't broken.

"You'll be plum-coloured tomorrow," I said. "Miss Plum, the Grocer's Daughter. That's you."

Julie loves Happy Families. I hate all card games, but I especially hate Happy Families. Still, I play it with her sometimes, like when she is sick.

"Master Plaster, the Doctor's Son," she said, with a snivel and a little grin.

"Nah, you don't need a plaster," I said. "You need an ice pack. Which we don't have. Or a packet of frozen peas, which we even more don't have."

"Peas!" she murmured, as if she was talking about some fabulous, exotic, unattainable fruit. "I'd love some peas. And mashed potato."

"Don't!" I groaned.

"It was because of the apples," she said. "I was crying because apples make me hungry instead of filling me up, they make my tummy water, and that was why she . . ."

That wasn't why. It wasn't Julie's fault. But I just said, "Listen, I have some money. You and I are going out for a bag of chips, and then I will tuck you up in bed, and you don't have to go to school tomorrow, because of that face. How does that grab you?"

She brightened up at this. In fact, she lit up like a Christmas tree.

"No school?" she sang. "Really? Are you sure?"

"School's not so bad," I said.

Her face dropped.

"But I'm sure. You don't need to go. In fact, you *can't* go to school looking like that, you'd frighten the children!"

It was touch and go. Was she going to burst into tears again, or would she think it was funny? I grinned like a lunatic to indicate that humour was the correct response.

She got it. "Yay!" she said, and smiled.

She put her fingers very carefully to the tender place.

The nails were all bitten down.

"Don't touch it," I said, lifting her down off the table. "You'll only make it worse."

"I wish . . ." she said, and then stopped.

"Yeah," I said. "I know."

I knew what she wished because I wished it too. We wished we could go to Gramma's.

chapter two

"Jono?"

I woke up out of a dream of snakes, with my breath stuck in my neck. I was never so glad to wake up, but still, it was half past four in the morning.

"For the love of God, Julie," I hissed. "It's the middle of the night. What do you want? You haven't . . . ?"

She's not a bed wetter, Julie, not really, but she has the odd lapse when Ma gets extra ratty.

"No," she said, and stamped her bare foot, all indignation.

"OK, OK," I said. "So what is it? Nightmare?"

"No. Let me into your bed, I'm freezing."

"Julie," I said. "I can't do that."

"Why not?"

"It's not right. We're too old for that sort of thing."

"I am only eight."

"Yes, but I'm a big boy now. Boys and girls . . . brothers and sisters . . . don't . . ."

"That's just stupid," she said, and she climbed in at the foot of my bed, since I wouldn't let her in at the top, and put her two icy feet on my calves.

I closed my eyes.

"Jono," she said, "I have an idea."

"Hmmm?" I said, turning over. I didn't want to encourage her.

"Let's run away."

"Go back to your own bed, Julie."

"Why don't we run away?"

"Because . . . oh, Julie, don't be silly."

"I'm not. I was reading this book and these children ran off to an island and they made cocoa and they weaved baskets for raspberries. They had a cow."

"Oh yeah?" I said. "Sounds dead practical. And it's *wove*."

She giggled and wriggled her feet in under my legs. "Wove!" she said. "Wove, wove, wove." She made it sound like a ridiculous word. "Oh wove, wovie, wove, wove-a-doodle, wivvy-wove-wovie."

"Shut up. Go back to bed. Your feet are warm now – if you run they won't have time to get cold again."

"My face hurts," she said in a whiny voice. "It's weally sohe, Jonathan."

She used not to be able to pronounce the letter *R*, and she still does it when she's looking for sympathy.

With a sigh, I turned on the bedside lamp. Her face was pale and blotched. I thought I could see the bruised part throbbing, but that might have been a trick of the light.

"I'll get you some medicine," I said.

I pushed my legs out of the bed and padded to the bathroom in the dim light that we left on overnight on the landing because Julie is scared of the dark.

I looked in the bathroom cabinet. None of the Calpol stuff Ma gives her when she's sick.

I fingered a packet of paracetamol and pressed one tablet out of its blister. I snapped it in half and sloshed some tap water into a glass.

I wondered if it was OK to give a child even half a tablet. I couldn't read the instructions in the semi-darkness, but I felt reluctant to turn on the bathroom light. I think I thought that if I kept the lights off, then Ma wouldn't wake up. Which made no sense, because her bedroom door was closed. I just felt safer in the yellowy night-light.

I went back into my room, but Julie'd fallen asleep, so I didn't have to poison her after all with the quarter dose of paracetamol.

I left the door to my room half open and went and slept in her bed. It was all rumpled and uncomfortable, and it smelled of her little-girl strawberry smell, and the duvet was too thin. No wonder she was cold.

chapter three

One time when I was not much older than Julie is now, I ran away. Not all by myself. Me and Granda, see, we went off together.

It was his idea. He was a madman, now I come to think of it, but when you are only a kid, you don't notice that kind of thing, do you? You just think adults are all much the same and know stuff you don't know. It doesn't occur to you that some of them might be loo-lah.

He was a right one, was Granda. He'd got this idea they were trying to kill him, and the only one he could trust was me. So one day, when Gramma was out shopping and I was in their house for some reason, I can't remember why, he made me put his things in a wheelie suitcase. I remember what I packed. A bottle of whisky wrapped in a bath towel, a pack of cards, a small radio, his very worst pair of slippers that he wasn't allowed to wear at home and a handful of assorted clothes that he just pitched out of a drawer and into the suitcase. He never thought of clothes for me; nor did I.

"That's the way they pack in the films," he said. "Not if they are going on a holiday then they pack normally. But if they are running away, they just open a drawer and dump stuff in a suitcase. I've always wanted to do that."

"Why?" I wanted to know.

"It seems so glamorous," he said.

Glamorous was not a word that sprang to mind when I looked at Granda. He hadn't shaved for two days and the front of his shirt had got caught in the zip of his fly.

"Are we running away?" I asked.

"Course we are."

"Where are we going?" I asked.

"Ask me no questions . . ." he said.

He didn't finish the sentence, but I knew it went, "and I'll tell you no lies." Even at ten, I knew this was a very unsatisfactory answer to a reasonable question.

We set off for the bus stop. First off, Granda said he'd just take his stick, he didn't want his walking frame, couldn't manage it with the suitcase anyway. But as soon as we were out of the estate and on to the footpath of the main road, he decided he needed the frame after all.

"Sit there, young fella," he said – he never called me by my name, sometimes I wonder if he even knew it, he just called me "young fella". He used his stick to turn the suitcase on its side and he poked me in the groin to make me sit.

I stumbled and fell backwards on top of the suitcase.

"I'll be back," he said, and off he went, into the estate again. I sat for ages on the suitcase, and fended off what felt like dozens of nosy old women who wanted to know if I was going on my holidays or what?

At last I heard Granda coming wheezing along, going *shuffle-clunk, shuffle-clunk*, on the frame.

"How are you going to get on the bus with that thing, Granda?" I asked when he came up to me.

He scowled, as if I'd asked a rude question.

"I've been on the bus dozens of times," he said regally. "Dozens of times."

"Yeah, but not on your frame," I said.

"Course I have," he said.

I couldn't remember a single time he'd done that, but he was a grown-up and I was a kid, so I said, "OK."

The bus driver took one look at us and threw his eyes up.

A black lady that was waiting at the bus stop with us took the suitcase for me, so I could concentrate on Granda. I'll never forget it. I had to take the frame from him and put it on the bus and then come back for him. He started yelling at me that I shouldn't have taken the frame, and he made me go back for it. So I had to walk down the aisle of the bus again and retrieve the frame from the luggage compartment, where I'd just managed to squeeze it in, and bring it to the door of the bus, and of course he couldn't lever himself up with it, he couldn't reach it from the pavement, so then he started shouting at me to take the bloody frame away.

I was fit to be tied and dead embarrassed too; we were holding everyone up. I wanted to yell at him that that's what I had done in the first place, that I'd been right and he'd been wrong, but Granda was never wrong. Never.

So I went back through the bus again with the frame and stuck it into the luggage space under the steps, and then I came back to the door and somehow I managed to haul Granda on. A man got out of his seat and helped me to manoeuvre Granda into it.

"Thank you," I kept saying, first to the man who had given up his seat to Granda, and then to the black woman who was bringing up the rear with the suitcase.

Granda didn't say thank you to anyone. He just gave this important-looking little wave, like the Pope.

There was no room for the suitcase in the luggage area because the frame was in it, stuck at an awkward angle with its little rubber feet in the air. Also, the long handle for rolling the suitcase with had stuck, which made it even more awkward to manage. The woman was still hanging on to it.

"Would any of yous be thinking of paying yiser fares?" the bus driver yelled at us down the bus.

"I haven't paid a fare for twenty years," Granda shouted back at him.

"Yeah, you look it an' all," said the driver. "But the boy has to pay."

"He's with me," said Granda grandly.

"He still has to pay."

I was scarlet by this time. I just wanted to disappear.

I stood up and leaned over the suitcase handle, which was at about nose height for me, and I thrust a hot little bundle of coins into the black lady's hand.

"Would you pay my fare for me?" I said.

"Where you going, lad?" she said.

"I dunno," I said. "Where are we going, Granda?"

"Kingsbridge," said Granda.

"Never heard of it," said the bus driver.

"Are you Polish or what?" asked my grandfather.

"From Roscommon," said the driver. But he wasn't. You could tell by the accent, he was from Ballyfermot or somewhere. He was kidding.

"Jeez-uss!" said Granda. "If it isn't foreigners, it's bleedin' boggers."

I elbowed him and tried to make a gesture to say the kind lady that had helped with the suitcase was foreign and not to be so rude, but he didn't care.

"He means Heuston Station," said an oul' one. "I agree witcha," she said, turning to Granda. "I never can remember either. I always have to stop and think which station is which. They had a right not to change them."

"They did that in 1966," muttered another oul' one. "It's time you got used to it."

I couldn't get my head around the idea of 1966. That's the last century. It's, like, decades ago, lifetimes back. I was trying to subtract 1966 from the year we were in, and I couldn't manage it.

"Is this bus ever going to move?" a woman asked. "Some of us have work to go to."

She didn't look as if she was going to work. She was all dolled up as if she was going to a party. Maybe she was a model or something.

"I'm not going to Heuston," said the driver. "I'll take yiz into town. Yous can get a Luas from there."

"A tram, he means," Granda said to the ol' one who'd explained about Kingsbridge. "God, wouldn't you just wish they'd leave the bloody language alone and not be monkeying about with the names of everything? It's disgraceful what's going on."

"It's true for you," said the ol' one, delighted to have met an old codger as bad as herself.

The woman who'd mentioned 1966 threw her eyes up, and I could hear her thinking, "Get a life," though she didn't say it.

The black woman paid the fare and brought me my ticket and change, where I was still trapped on my seat behind the jammed handle of the suitcase. She gave me an encouraging little wink, but I didn't feel very encouraged.

I can't remember how we got off, but we had no trouble with the Luas. I remember thinking they should manufacture more buses the same as the Luases with nice flat floors. Some of them are like that, but you can't count on it.

We queued up for ages at the ticket window at the train station. It must have been rush hour or something, because the station was full of people and the queues snaked nearly out as far as the platform from the window where they sell the tickets.

Granda had an old person's travel pass, but he still needed a ticket, and he needed to have a row with them too about my ticket. He wasn't planning to pay for it. He was entitled to bring a companion on his pass, he said, and I was his companion.

I said I thought the companion had to be over sixteen. That was why I'd had to pay on the bus.

"That's ridiculous," he said. "I never heard such nonsense. I blame the government."

He was right there, I suppose.

"I don't think I could pass for sixteen," I said.

"Don't be absurd, boy," he said. "Of course you can't, you are only a runt of a child. But I'll have it out with them. Just you wait and see. I have no intention of paying a fare for a babe in arms."

"I'm not a babe in arms," I pointed out.

He scowled and said, "You know what I mean." But I didn't.

Anyway, it never came to that, because when we finally got to the top of the queue it turned out that Granda had brought Gramma's travel pass by mistake, and they wouldn't give him a ticket on it.

The ticket seller was a fat bloke with a pasty face. He looked like one of Gramma's cakes of soda bread before she put it in the oven. He had glasses that looked too big for his face, and he wore a creased-looking shirt in a pale colour.

He had a tie, but he'd left his collar open and the tie was knotted in the wrong place.

"But would you take a look at me!" Granda barked. "What age do you think I am?"

"I am sure you are a great age, sir," said the ticket seller pleasantly, pushing his glasses up his greasy nose with a fat forefinger, "but I doubt if you are Lulu Kinahan."

That was Gramma's name.

"It is irrelevant who I am. I am clearly of advanced years; therefore I am entitled to free travel, and I demand free travel."

"You are only entitled to free travel with a travel pass, sir," said the ticket man. He was still quite calm.

"And what do you call this?" Granda waved the pass at the window behind which the ticket man sat.

The ticket man actually smiled. "I call that somebody else's travel pass, sir," he said.

"And do you mean to tell me you are not going to give me a ticket on a technicality like that, you young pup, you?"

He didn't look young to me, but I suppose these things are relative.

"I don't think personation is a technicality," said the ticket man, beginning to lose his sense of humour, and his "sir", now I come to think of it.

"Personation?" Granda was rigid with indignation. "I am not impersonating anyone!"

"Well, you are trying to use someone else's travel pass," said the ticket man. "That's illegal. Next!"

He called the last word out loud, summoning the next person in the queue to come forward to buy their ticket.

"It's a bloody disgrace," my grandfather said, sagging over his frame and shaking his head. He should have been in a wheelchair, but you couldn't tell him anything.

All I could think of was the journey home we were going to have to make with the frame and the suitcase on the Luas and the bus, and the reception we were going to get when we arrived. I knew we weren't going anywhere now. Even if Granda had the money to pay for our train tickets, there was no way he was going to do it.

I was right. There was merry hell to pay when we got home.

Gramma was beside herself. I never did work out whether it was because she thought she'd never see her grandson again or her travel pass. It certainly had nothing to do with never seeing Granda again, that's for sure.

That kinda put me off running away from home, I have to admit. Actually, I didn't think Granda came into this story at all, but there you go, you never know how things are all connected, do you?

It's funny how when you look back, you see the points where, if you'd acted differently, you might have changed things, and everything might have turned out different. I'm not saying it was my fault or anything, or that I should have gone along with Julie's madcap idea and just stuck a few changes of underwear in a rucksack and legged it. You'd have had to be eight to think that was a good idea. Or seventy-eight. But if I *had*, then, who knows?

chapter four

Julie couldn't open her eye in the morning and her face was like a balloon on one side. I tried bathing it in cold water, but she kept screeching. I should have made ice overnight, but I didn't think of it. I never expected it would be so bad. I scraped some snowy stuff from the inside of the freezer into a cereal bowl using a soup spoon, and then poured it into a sandwich bag. I gave it to her wrapped in a tea towel and she hugged it carefully to her face.

Ma slept through all this, as usual. She didn't get up before noon any day. "I never drink until the afternoon," she used to boast, and it was true, but she had sherry for breakfast all the same.

Don't get me wrong, Ma wasn't always such a waste of space. I can remember a time before, when things were normal enough, and Da was home and we used to do family stuff like going to the zoo, that kinda shit. Good shit, you know. I remember Julie in her buggy and Da pushing it in the Phoenix Park and Ma with a flower in her hair and all laughing and stuff. I remember one night Da calling me in to look at Julie in her cot. She was asleep on her stomach with her bum in the air. Her nappy was making a little puffy bump under her babygro, and her knees were bent so that her legs were nearly tucked under her.

"Doesn't she look like a turkey?" Da whispered. "All trussed up for the oven."

The two of us had a good laugh about that, and then Da kissed his fingers and touched them to Julie's hair and she turned her head so that she was sleeping on the opposite cheek. You could see a big red patch where she'd been resting on it just a moment ago. We turned out the light then and left the room.

I don't know where Ma was that night, the night Da said Julie looked like a turkey. I'm not saying she wasn't round much in those days, because she must have been. I'd have noticed if she wasn't, but you don't remember every single little thing, do you? You just remember these little scenes, like me and Da in Julie's room, laughing at her asleep, only it wasn't laughing *at* her really, it was laughing because we loved her, the two of us, and we were glad we had her. And yet I remember the running-away-with-Granda story pretty clearly. Memory is weird.

I couldn't think what I was going to do with Julie. There was no way she could go to school looking like that. There'd be a social worker on the doorstep by lunchtime. (Why do the social workers take the children away? Why don't they take the parents? That'd be a much better idea. Residential care for troubled parents. That's brilliant – I should enter it in the Young Scientists.) But I couldn't leave her at home either, with no one to look after her.

"I'm hungry, Jonathan," she whined.

"Have an apple," I said heartlessly, and she started wailing.

"Oh, shut up and let me think," I said.

"I wish Gramma was here," she sniffed.

"If you had a tune for that, you could sing it," I said.

"What does that mean?" she asked, still holding the wet cold tea towel to her face.

"It means yeah, yeah," I said.

The only thing, I decided, was for me to skip school as well.

I wasn't going to just mitch off, though. They'd be on to me like a shot. And I couldn't say I was sick. I'd done that the previous week, and there's a limit to how often you can be sick without people getting suspicious. They are dead suspicious in my school. I don't know what ever happened to trust.

So I rang the school secretary and said I wouldn't be in because my ma was sick and she was so bad I couldn't leave her on her own. I hadn't used that one before, because I don't like to draw attention to Ma. I said she had the winter vomiting bug. I don't know what that is exactly but it sounds awful and nobody wants to know you if you have come anywhere near it, so I reckoned I'd be good for a few days on that one. Also, it was true in a kind of way. It was winter and she had been vomiting.

There was still no food in the house, only the apples, so I stole into Ma's room and took a twenty-euro note out of her jeans pocket. I was amazed that she had it. If she'd had all that money, how come she'd only brought apples home for dinner? I *knew* how come, and for a moment I could feel the anger rising through my bloodstream, but I told myself, *Don't waste your energy, Jono.*

I was tempted to blow it all on Coco Pops and Mars bars, but I was very responsible. I bought brown bread and milk and some of those yogurt drinks. Also some Calpol. You would not believe what that stuff costs.

"What did you get?" Julie asked when I came back from the shop.

"Bread," I said. "We're having apple sandwiches for breakfast."

"Apple sandwiches?" She sounded dubious.

"Yeah, it's what they eat in all the best houses," I said.

"Do they really?" she asked.

"Well, only on the mornings when they have apples left over from dinner the day before," I said.

"I see," she said solemnly.

Kids don't get jokes. I kinda like that about Julie, the way she is so thick about jokes, but sometimes you could do with a bit of audience appreciation, know what I mean?

The apple sandwiches weren't half bad, but I was afraid it would hurt Julie's face to chew. She ate it all up, though, and drank some milk. I felt ridiculously proud of her. Or maybe of myself.

I have this girlfriend. Sort of. Well, we like each other, but we're not exactly going out together.

Anyway, me and Annie – her name is Annie, did I say that before? – we just phone each other in the evenings, and we have a lot of laughs, but when we actually meet, we're a bit shy with each other. Or I am anyway. Her brother Jamie is my best friend at school, even though he's a year ahead of me. It's because they used to live next door to us. She has the shiniest hair you ever saw, and her face is wide open. She plays the clarinet. Isn't that something? The *clarinet*. She says she's going to join the army band when she's older. I said that means she has to be a soldier, but she just shrugs at that. She doesn't really see beyond this idea of herself with sparkly bits marching around tooting on her clarinet, the mad eejit.

She's in my year at school, only in a different class, because her surname starts with W. So she wouldn't necessarily notice if I wasn't at school, but I sent her a text anyway. I didn't say too much, just said I'd be out for a while. She's cool. She won't come running around with a thermometer or anything. But I wouldn't just say nothing, or then she really might come around, to see if we're all right. She worries about Julie, I think.

Julie was hanging in there, though. All she wanted now was to watch something on the telly, but of course, as usual, there was nothing on. I can hear Gramma saying, in her prissy way that was supposed to be funny, "Actually, there is a whole lot of stuff on the telly. There is nothing that anyone with an IQ above that of an undereducated wood louse would care to watch, but that is another matter."

She talked like that, she really did. She was sound, Gramma. I was cracking up laughing to myself just thinking about her. She used to wear these mad clothes, all too big for her because she was so skinny, and all clashing colours. She did it on purpose to be eccentric. I think if you are really eccentric you don't do it on purpose, but Gramma made a kind of hobby out of it. Lulu Fortycoats the neighbours called her. That was partly because her maiden name was Fortescue, which they thought was a bit uppity and needed taking down a peg. That's what Gramma said anyway. I think it's a nice name.

Well, to cut a long story short, because this is supposed to be some kind of a story even though it is true, we muddled through like that for a day or two, eating apple sandwiches and potatoes. I forgot to mention the potatoes. I bought them in the evening, with what was left of the money and a few coins I found down the back of the sofa, and we had them mashed with curry powder. You'd be amazed how far a bag of potatoes can take you. That's what caused the famine, I know, eating potatoes, but I don't think two days of it would kill you.

It was like a kind of daft holiday. We pretended we were just having a good time, and we tried not to think about all the *stuff*. Ma kept out of our way – tell the truth, I think she was a bit embarrassed about hitting Julie – so we could do more or less what we liked. We ate our potatoes in the sitting room because the kitchen was too cold, and Ma had worked out some way of tapping into the electricity so that you didn't have to pay for the electric fire. I'm sure it was dangerous and I know it was illegal, but at least we didn't freeze.

The day after that was dole day, so I got Ma out of bed and brushed her down and sent her off to collect the money. I know I am making it sound as if she was in bed for three days solid, which is not true, but I am just moving along here.

I remember when I was littler, when Da first left and before Gramma realized what was going on here, Ma used to forget to get the dole money. She'd just sleep through until I came home from school and it was too late and then there'd be nothing to eat.

I started acting up at school then on dole days, so that they'd have to send me home. One day I pretended I was choking and the teacher had to do a thing called the Hindenberg manoeuvre, only it's not Hindenberg exactly, which basically means beating you up until you stop. And then they didn't even send me home, just made me lie down for a little while. That was the worst day of my life, lying on a little pull-out sofa thing in the secretary's office looking at those horrible ceiling tiles with all the holes in them – they look sort of medical or something – and wishing I could just go home and get Ma up. But they wouldn't let me go home; they said there might be something stuck in my soft guts (I thought that's what they said, it was *oesophagus*, I know that now) and it would be dangerous to send me home.

So the next week I wet myself, and would you believe it? They just gave me clean things to wear. That was when I realized that no matter how miserable I made myself at school, they weren't going to send me home. And I did not like sitting around all day in somebody else's underpants. So I started really acting up then, rampaging around the classroom, spitting and shrieking and pulling people's hair. I thought, They'll definitely send me home now, maybe they'll even expel me, but they just put me in a quiet room and got this counsellor person to come and talk to me, but I didn't want to talk to anyone. I didn't want anyone finding out anything about me or my family, so I pretended I had a speech defect – you know, like when you can't talk properly.

In the end, I worked out a much simpler method. You mess about in class, you talk, you are disruptive, but not so bad they think you need counselling, just so bad they think your behaviour is terrible, so then they take you to the principal's office and they ring your mother, to embarrass you, I suppose.

And then there's this long, long, long wait until eventually Ma answers the phone, and you are imagining her rolling out of bed, cursing, and tumbling down the stairs in her pyjamas and still cursing.

There'd be all this hugger-muggering when she answered, and then I'd say, "Can I talk to her for a minute please?" so they'd give me the phone, and I'd cup my hand over the mouthpiece and whisper, "Ma, you need to go and get the stuff, you know?" like a person in a gangster movie talking about drugs or guns or something, and she would giggle and say, "I'm just on my way, guv'nor."

At least, she used to giggle at first, she thought it was a gas the way I would get them to ring up, but after a while she started getting belligerent about it and then she would snarl into the phone and make all these threats and ask me who did I think I was telling her what to do. I'd be standing there in the principal's office with my finger stuck over the place on the receiver where the voice comes out, in case anyone heard the stuff she was yelling at me. It was like a kind of verbal vomit: it stank and you couldn't make it stop.

Then I got a mobile phone and it was a whole lot easier, especially when I started at secondary school, where you can nip out between classes to make a phone call.

Life is much better as you get older. The younger you are, the harder it is. Secondary school is much better than primary school for other reasons too. You are not stuck in a classroom with one adult all day long. Even if you don't like one class, you can always look forward to the next one. Lots of things like that. And they leave you alone more. They don't seem to feel they have to monitor every thought you have.

chapter five

After three days the bottle of Calpol was nearly empty and Julie's face was still livid. The girl who walked into doors.

They rang from her school to know where she was. I couldn't believe I'd been so stupid. I was so concerned about spinning my own school a yarn and texting Annie and all that I'd forgotten Julie would need an excuse too.

"Eh – she's got the – the whatchamacall it, the winter vomiting bug," I said.

Not the optimum answer, but all I could come up with on the spot. She'd been out three days. It would be stretching it a bit to keep her at home much longer with a thing like that. I should have invented some really long illness for her, to give her time for her face to heal. Scarlet fever or mumps or something. Measles. I could check the internet, if only I could get out to the library, but Julie wouldn't stay in the house on her own with Ma, and I couldn't risk taking her with me. I could always ring Annie and ask her to check it for me, but then I'd have to explain it all to her, and she . . . well, it's not that I couldn't trust her, but it wouldn't be fair to land all this stuff on her. It was too late now anyway, since I'd mentioned the vomiting thing.

"Oh," said the person who'd rung. I forget who it was, if I'd ever heard. "That's too bad. Is she nearly better?"

"No," I said. "It's a bad case." Inspiration hit me. "She got dehydrated. They had to put her on a drip. She was in hospital overnight. Terrible it was."

I was dead proud of that little detail. Mr O'Connell is always telling us to put in "telling detail". It convinces your reader, he says. And he was right. Your woman at the other end of the phone swallowed my story, hook, line and sinker. Maybe the ideal reader is a fish after all.

"Dear me," said the voice. "Could I speak to your mother?"

"She's sick too," I said. "We've all had it. She can't come to the phone."

"Dear, oh dear," said the voice again. "And how about you, are you OK?"

"Walking wounded," I said with a short laugh, to show I was putting on a brave face.

"Is there anything we can do? Could I drop over

some soup or something?"

"No, no," I said, "my grandmother . . ."

"I thought she'd passed away?"

"The other one," I muttered, wishing to God I could just hang up.

"Oh, well, that's good. You mind yourself, now, young man. Jonathan, isn't it? Give Julie our best regards. Tell her we all miss her. I'll ring again in a day or two if she doesn't show up."

"Thanks," I said. "And sorry for not ringing."

After I'd hung up, I realized my hands were shaking.

I'd really messed up. I should have said she'd had a fall or something, brazened it out from the start. It was going to be ages before she was fit to be seen, and I couldn't see how I could keep her under wraps for much longer. And now I'd invented an illness, multiplied by three, a hospital stay *and* a living grandmother. Keep it simple, they say, if you must lie. Great advice, but not that easy to follow.

I was going to have to go back to school myself pretty swiftish too, or the home-school liaison officer would be on my case. She's all right, actually, old Ma Leary, but I don't want anyone, even a very nice person, coming nosing in here and saying Julie has to go off to some foster home or something. Whatever happens, I thought, I have to keep Julie with me. I wasn't going to let anyone get their paws on her. She was mine. But how the hell was I going to do that?

I was sitting there on the sofa, trying to think it all through, when this *peep-peep* sound came from under a magazine on the coffee table. *Peep-peep* it went again.

I lifted the magazine, and there was Julie's mobile phone under it. I hate that thing. I don't think eight-year-olds should have mobiles, if you ask me. They should be tumbling with puppies and climbing trees, not playing Pac-Man on *pink* phones. Call me old-fashioned, but there it is.

Idly, I opened the message. I don't know what possessed me. I never open people's mail or anything. I think I did it automatically. I was sitting with a phone in my hand and the message icon was showing, so I just opened it without thinking. This was the message that some monster kid had sent to Julie:

hey jool we no yer mas a alco
wer gonna get u when u cum bak
2 skool u scum

I sat there with the stupid phone in my hand, and all I could think was, She's only eight, she's only eight. Who under God could do this to an eight-year-old *child*? Scum!

I could hardly breathe, I was so angry. I jabbed frantically to delete the horrible message, muttering, "Scum yourself, you sorry little bitch." The only person who could send a message like that to an eight-year-old, I thought, was another eight-year-old, and I was pretty sure it was that awful Danielle creature she hangs out with. I know her brother, he's a pukeball. For two pins I'd have gone around to their rotten little prissy house with its cobblelock drive and its flowery curtains matching in all the windows and knocked her smirky little self-satisfied head off.

I could hear the toilet flushing upstairs. That was Julie. I forgot to say Ma had been out all that evening.

I turned the phone off. I didn't want it ringing or beeping. Maybe Julie would think she'd lost it. I put it in my pocket. I could hear her coming down the stairs now. She always comes down the way little kids do. First one foot on the step, then the other, then the first foot on the next step, and so on, planting two feet on each step before the next one. She's big enough to come down the proper way. I think she just does it because she likes it. She sings as she comes downstairs, some song about coming downstairs.

I sat for a long time in the sitting room, with that phone in my pocket lying like a bar of venom against my thigh. What the hell was I going to do?

After I'd packed Julie off to bed, I sent a text message to that filthy little turd, Danielle Butler. I got the number off Julie's phone, but I sent it from my own phone. This is what I wrote (and by the way, I use predictive text, none of that lazy old *B4* rubbish for me):

If you lay a hand on my sister, you little bitch, I will personally come and beat you till you are black and blue and your teeth rattle in your poxy little head. Scum yourself. I know where you live. JK

I had no intention of doing anything to her, I wouldn't hurt a fly, and she is only eight, but I needed her to feel how scary it is when someone sends you a message like that. Poxy little cow.

Then I sat for ages in the dark, with my head in a swirl. My thoughts were spinning round and round, like clothes in a washing machine. Bruise, I thought. Alcoholic. Social worker. Foster care. Scum. School. Measles. Cow. Mobile phone. Danielle.

Then the thoughts started to swirl faster. We were in the spin cycle now. Foster bruise. Social school. The sleeves were wrapping themselves round the collars, the washing ball had worked its way into a pocket, a glove fingered the toe of a sock. Scum school. Alco social. Danielle. Foster phone. Bruise cow.

I was drifting into sleep.

You probably think I hate Ma, but I didn't hate her. I didn't have the energy for hatred, and anyway I was too busy trying to keep everything together for Julie. But that's not why I don't hate her.

She's my mother.

I heard a woman in a supermarket once telling the checkout person she was buying the food for her mother's funeral. "Ah God," said the checkout girl. "I'm sorry to hear that. You only have one mother, isn't that the way?"

That *is* the way. You don't get to pick your parents, but

once you're landed with them, that's it. And there's no good in hating them, it only leads to awfulness.

Mind you, the awfulness happens anyway, all by itself. You don't need to do a thing.

In some ways my da was worse. I mean, he never hit us or anything, but by God he ruled our house with an iron fist all the same. We couldn't get to do stuff, just normal stuff, like play soccer or take a part in the school play or join the Boy Scouts. I mean, yeah, in theory we could. There wasn't a rule against it or anything. That'd be easier, like the Mormon kid we had in my class for a while; he couldn't do stuff because his family had these rules. But rules you can handle, even shitty ones like that. It's when you think there's no problem, and you sign up for something and you come home and you tell them, all excited, that you've been picked to play soccer for the school or you've been put on the quiz team or whatever, and everyone's thrilled for you, and beaming, and banging you on the back, and then suddenly you do something you didn't even know was wrong, like you leave a door open or you drop your socks into the linen basket without turning them the right way out, and *wham*! No soccer practice, or quiz team, or Boy Scouts meeting, or rehearsals for you, my boy, you've got to learn to *behave*. In the end, you get the message and you just don't sign up for anything, see, because no matter what it is, you are going to end up not being allowed to take part.

I never understood why. It was just always like that. You accepted it, or you didn't, and in the end, you worked out that accepting it was much the easier option.

Ma had learned that ages ago. She'd learned to keep her trap shut. But the thing is, she ended up not even trying to protect us. We had to stand up to Da or we had to give in to him. She just didn't get involved anymore.

I had a birthday party once. I was seven, I think, and Da was away, so Ma said, Sure, you can have a party. It was just a normal party, with jelly – purple jelly and ice cream and Pass the Parcel and those feathery things you blow, and everyone said it was the best party they had ever been to, real old-fashioned, with the sandwiches and everything, nobody ever had sandwiches at parties anymore. It was mostly Gramma who organized it, so I suppose that's why it was so old-fashioned, because of course she was old, being a grandmother. I remember she wanted to make the sandwiches with brown bread, but Ma said the kids would never stand for that, so in the end she gave in and when the party started there were all these beautiful little triangular sandwiches, all white and gleaming, but when you picked one up, the bottom triangle of bread was brown, so she pulled a fast one and got at least half the amount of brown bread into the kids, and she made everyone finish the sandwiches before the fairy cakes came out, and then the purple jelly. It was the best day of my life, and Ma really enjoyed it too. Julie was in her high chair banging her spoon on the tray and singing Happy Burrday, Happy Burrday dear JonTHAN, and we were all having a riot, and this boy called Keith Butler was shooting lumps of jelly off his spoon and landing them on the wall. He was taking bets on which lump would slither to the floor first. Only then my da came home unexpectedly and opened the kitchen door and a wet gob of purple jelly landed right on his forehead and he let this bawl out of him, like a bull having its nose ring pulled, and children scattered, screaming, under the table, out the back door, one lad even climbed up on the sink, God knows why. It would have been funny if it hadn't been so scary.

He didn't do that rage thing all that often. Most of the time he was grand. Even good fun sometimes. And he adored Julie. He used to throw her up in the air to make her scream with laughter and then catch her and swing her and throw her up again, and Ma would be pleading with him to be careful, he'd make Julie sick, or he'd drop her and break her, and I'd be jumping up beside him and begging him to throw me up in the air too, but of course I was far too big for that. I don't think he ever did it when I was small either.

I have never been able to work out if Ma started drinking because Da left, or if Da left because Ma started drinking. But now I think maybe it was all more complicated than that.

chapter six

Julie got a right surprise in the morning when she woke up to find me creeping about her bedroom.

I'd tipped the books out of her school bag, and I was bundling clothes in.

"What are you doing?" she hissed.

"Sssh," I said. "Don't want to wake Ma."

"Yes, but what are you doing?" This time she spoke in an even louder whisper.

"Packing," I said, and I held my hand out in front of me, palm side down, and lowered it repeatedly to indicate that she should bring the volume down.

She sat up in bed and hugged herself.

"But that's my school bag," she said. "And why are you patting the air like that?"

"Well, you haven't got another rucksack," I said. "And keep it down, will you?"

"What about *your* rucksack?" she asked.

"Packed already," I said.

"Jonathan! Are we . . ."

"Yes," I said. "You were right all along, Julie. I should have listened to you in the first place."

"Oh, wow!" she said, and leaped out of bed. She flung herself at me and threw her skinny little arms around my waist. "You are the best brother ever!"

"Yeah, I know," I said. "And you're pretty cool too. Come on now, get dressed and eat up your brekkie, so I can pack the teethbreesh."

She giggled. That was Gramma's word. She always said the plural of *toothbrush* should be *teethbreesh*. "In *fact*," she would say, in this professorial way she had, "the singular should be teethbrush anyway. Except for persons unlucky enough to have only one tooth."

"Come on, Julie," I said as she finished her breakfast. "Time to go."

I knew I had to get out of that house.

She smiled at me, but her face had gone very white. The parts of it that were not purple, I mean. The enormity of it all had suddenly hit her, I suppose.

"Where are we going to go?" she asked.

I hadn't a clue. I'd lain awake all night thinking about it, but I still hadn't got past step one. Even the longest journey has to start with a single step, I said to myself. Isn't that very wise of me, now? Actually, I read that somewhere. Probably on a calendar.

"First, we're going over to Gramma's house," I said.

Actually, I wasn't sure whose house it was now. Maybe the Corpo owned it. But I still had the key, and it's only three weeks since she died. I couldn't imagine that the Corpo would have moved in on it already, not with all the houses there are lying empty these days. The country is full of them. One more isn't going to make all that difference.

"We can't go to *Gramma's*," Julie said, her eyes wide.

"You can wear your hood up," I said. "If you keep close to me, no one will see."

Even though it had been days now since she'd got that blow, her face was still an awful colour. In fact, the bruise looked bigger and darker than it had at first, and it was shiny.

"It's *haunted*," she said.

I laughed. "Why would it be haunted?"

"Because," said Julie flatly.

She always says that when she doesn't know what else to say, but she says it with great conviction. You'd nearly think she'd said something sensible.

"Listen," I said. "Remember Gramma's steak and kidney pies?"

"Yeah," said Julie with sudden enthusiasm. She loves her grub.

"I wouldn't be surprised if there are a few of those still in her freezer."

"We can't *steal* stuff out of Gramma's freezer!" Julie sounded shocked.

"It wouldn't be stealing. She made them for us. And they don't belong to anyone anymore, right?"

That started Julie snivelling, but I ignored her. I didn't have time for arguments or emotional scenes.

"Come on now, Julie," I said. "Chop, chop. Go and choose a book, and then we're off. And a teddy."

Julie slipped obediently from her chair and padded off to her room.

"Make it a good book," I called up the stairs after her.

"Don't shout!" she said, appearing at the top of the stairs with a book under one arm and a teddy under the other and her finger to her lips. "You'll wake Ma."

She came down the stairs in that little-girl way that she should have grown out of by now, and she pushed her stuff into the top of her rucksack.

"I'm too big for teddies," she assured me.

"Then why did you bring one?"

"Because you *said*, Jonathan," she answered, all sweet reason.

"Oh, yeah. Right. I'm the boss, then?"

"Not of the family," she said. "And not of me.

Only of this trip."

Trip. She made it sound like a holiday.

I made Julie put on her warmest coat, but it didn't have a hood, so she had to take it off and put on a hoodie underneath. Then we wriggled our arms through our rucksack straps and hauled them onto our backs. I wound two scarves around Julie's neck. I had no idea how cold we were going to be, but I knew it wasn't going to be picnic weather out there anyway.

Julie was right in a way. It was kinda spooky going into Gramma's. We hadn't been there since the day of the funeral. It was freezing. Cold as the grave, I remember thinking. Not a good thought under the circumstances.

There was only one steak and kidney pie and it wasn't cooked, so we had to defrost it first and then cook it. The electricity was still on, luckily, so we micro*wove* it – another Gramma word – and then baked it in the oven. Gramma always had this theory that if the oven is on, the kitchen is warm, but her kitchen was still freezing even while the pie was cooking. Maybe it had got so cold you couldn't warm it up with just the oven being on.

The smell was fantastic though. I had a hard time keeping Julie from eating it all up on the spot. She'd been living on potatoes and apples for too long.

"That's tonight's dinner," I explained. "If you eat it now, you will still be hungry at dinner time. So best to hang on. Have a slice of bread."

There was bread in the freezer too, which we toasted to make it edible. And I found two loaves of her special banana cake with walnuts and ginger, which I wrapped in tea towels and packed for later, but the bread we laid into immediately.

I went rummaging through her stuff then, opening drawers and presses, not looking for anything in particular, but just in case there was something useful. I found a few coins, and her travel pass. I didn't think that'd be much good to us – neither of us looked like Lulu Kinahan, aged seventy-nine.

"I remember this!" Julie called, holding up a purple velvet hat with a feather. "And this!" she added, waving a game of Monopoly in the air. "Can we play, Jonathan?"

"Not now, Julie," I said. If there is one thing I hate more than Happy Families, it's Monopoly. "Listen now, I need you to be a brave girl. I have to go to the post office to get out the money in my savings book, and I want you to stay here and keep as quiet as a mouse. Can you manage that?" I thought she might start whining again about the house being haunted, but she must have got over that.

"I have savings too," she said. "My Communion money."

I wished she'd thought of that before we left home, but I didn't fancy going back to pick up her post office book, so I said, "You hold on to that, Julie. You'll need it when you get married."

I was only joking about getting married, but she nodded and said, "Oh, yeah. For my veil, right?"

"For sure," I said. "Who would you like to marry?"

"You," she said.

"Yeah, but I'll be married already," I said. "Who else? A prince?"

"No. A daddy."

"I see," I said.

I had forty-seven quid in the post office. I'd been saving for an iPod, like, forever. By the time I'd got enough money, they would be out of date, so I didn't really mind taking it out to fund our "trip", as Julie called it.

While I was out of the house, I sent a long text to Annie. She'd rung me the previous night, and when I saw her name coming up on the screen, I left the phone down on my bed and let it ring and ring and ring. But I couldn't just ignore her. First of all, I didn't want to hurt her feelings, and secondly, if I started acting strange, she'd probably start getting suspicious. So I sent her a long funny text about nothing much, and I never said a word about what was going on. That'd buy me a day or two anyway, I thought, and just then I couldn't think ahead in blocks of time any longer than twenty-four hours.

"Can we go to Daddy's house?" Julie asked when I got back with the moola.

"No," I said. "That would be the last place we should go."

Because of course it was the first place they'd go to find us.

"I *want* to go to Daddy's," she whined.

She didn't really. She wanted to go to the daddy she had made up for herself, not the da we really had, because the da we really had was someone else's daddy now. He wouldn't be one bit pleased to see his other children. That was us, the other children, which is weird, because we were there first, but somehow, that's how it had turned out.

"I love Daddy," Julie said, though I knew she couldn't possibly remember him, not really. She might have a few vague impressions, but that was the height of it.

"Hmmm," I said. "You know, that's not a good idea, Julie. We need to keep away from Da, because that's where they'll think we've gone."

"So what?" she said. "Doesn't matter if they find us, does it? Not if we are with Daddy. We can tell them Ma hit me, so we had to leave, and that'll be OK, won't it, 'cos you're not supposed to hit your children, are you?"

I wished it was as simple as she thought.

I was packing the banana cakes and the rest of the bread into my rucksack, along with the pie, which was still hot.

"Well," I said, "tell you what. We'll start out in the general direction of where Da lives. We'll go to Galway. And we can decide later if we want to actually hook up with him. We might be happy enough on our own. We mightn't want to be bothered with him. Not if we are getting on fine and all."

That really was weird logic. I was thinking as straight as I could, but maybe that was not all that very straight. But it seemed to appeal to her. I think it was the idea that we could decide. We didn't have to do anything unless we wanted to.

"Fuck it and see?" she said.

I was shocked. No, really. She's only a kid. What kind of *sluts* was she hanging about with? That bloody Danielle Butler and her rotten little cronies.

Then I got it, and I laughed.

"*Suck* it, Julie. Like a lollipop – you suck it to see if you like it. That's what it means."

"Yeah, yeah," she said, "same difference."

chapter seven

It would have been nice to go by train, but I knew the bus was a lot cheaper, so we set off for Busáras, which, by the way, has to be the draughtiest place in Ireland. I mean, if you design a place with five thousand doors, and they are all open, it is going to be bloody cold, isn't it? Like the Snow Queen's palace in the fairy tale, only it is the not-so-pretty version.

You would be amazed at some of the people who travel by bus. They look as if they need a decent pair of shoes, and their suitcases are tied up with blue twine (why would anyone invent twine that is *blue*?), and they talk without opening their mouths. The blokes that sell the tickets in Busáras don't understand them. They look blank when addressed in Closed Mouth, and they shake their heads and push their hats back, but it never seems to occur to them to say, *Would you ever open your mouth there, sonny, and I might have some chance of understanding you.*

Anyway, we found the Galway bus and we got seats at the front, where you can see out the window. There wasn't all that much to see for the first half of the journey, only scrubby fields that were very cold-looking and had sheep in them. I began to understand why sheep have so much wool. I've become a kind of expert on the cold lately.

The bus stopped for a while near Athlone, and we had a picnic of steak and kidney pie. Julie persuaded me that it would be OK to eat it even though it wasn't dinner time yet. It was still slightly warm, she said, and it would be an awful waste to wait until it was cold. She was right. It tasted delicious. Good old Gramma. And then we had an orange each that I had bought in a little kiosk place in Busáras, because, unlike Ma, I know about the food pyramid and I didn't want Julie getting rickets or scurvy or any of that kind of thing.

The other passengers had mostly got off the bus when it stopped, to go to the toilets or buy drinks and chocolate bars, and they all turned up their noses in disgust when they went past us on their way back to their seats and got the smell of oranges. I don't see why. I think it's a nice smell, although maybe not so great on a bus. But just to be neighbourly, I tucked the orange peel into a plastic bag and tied the top of it very tightly, so the orangey smell would be trapped inside. Very considerate of me, don't you think? That's me, all heart.

It was evening by the time we arrived in Galway, and I hadn't a clue what we should do next. We didn't have enough money for a B&B, and we hadn't thought to bring a tent, so we walked up and down the prom in Salthill a few times and pretended we were enjoying the sea air, but we were really freezing.

When it got too dark for that, we found a kind of wind shelter. It was better than being out in the wind, but only just, because it was made completely of concrete, which is the coldest material known to man, if you ask me. But I didn't say anything about the cold to Julie, and she didn't say anything to me either, though I could see her shivering under her rucksack.

We unpacked our sleeping bags, and I made Julie take off her coat and put on some more layers of clothes because I knew the cold of that concrete was going to seep into our bones. Then we got into our sleeping bags, and the two of us cuddled up together on the concrete bench and waited for the morning.

Julie opened her eyes just before dawn, and she said, "Why did we run away?"

"For fun," I said.

"Really?" she said sleepily. "Was that the reason?"

I traced her bruise very gently with my thumb. The

swelling had gone down a lot, but the colour was still dark.

"Oh, yeah," she said. "I forgot. It's because of my face, isn't it?"

"More or less," I said.

For the first time, it struck me that the cheekbone had probably been broken.

She went back to sleep, and I held her for the longest time. Her hair smelled fruity, from some daft shampoo that she uses, which would be more appropriate poured over a dessert, I always think.

"We need a cup of tea," I said when she woke up again. "I mean, two cups of tea."

"I don't drink tea," she said. "I don't like it."

"You do now," I said, "because I can't afford hot chocolate and you have to get something hot into you or you might get frostbite."

"Frostbite?" She wiggled her fingers speculatively, as if to check they were all intact. "Where? Where might I get frostbite? I can't feel my toes. Is that it? I don't think tea would be any good for your toes, would it?"

"I suppose you could pour it over them, to defrost them, like," I said, with a big grin to show I was only joking. You have to be clear about that kind of thing with Julie. Her sense of humour is a bit underdeveloped. I'd say living with Ma has stunted her in that department.

"Oooh," she said, but she didn't make any more objections to the tea.

We ran like frenzy up and down the beach to get warm before we went for our tea, but it didn't really work because our feet kept sinking in the sand and we couldn't get a good speed up. We just got sand in our shoes. It was a stupid idea to spend the night by the sea. Everyone knows it's the coldest place.

"We should've run on the footpath," Julie said. "Now our feet will hurt because the sand will rub the skin off."

"The prom, you call that path," I said. "Here, gimme your socks and I'll shake the sand out of them. We can't have your skin coming off."

When she took her socks off, I could see she was right about her toes being so cold. They were like frozen peas that had seen a ghost. I rubbed her feet to get the blood flowing, and I blew on them to get the last of the sand off and to warm them up.

After we'd had a long cup of tea in a little café, we went into the city and we walked about all day. We saw the boat that goes out to the Aran Islands. They have planes these days, for people and the mails, but I suppose there are things that are still better taken over there on a boat. Like if you bought furniture or something.

"Can we go to the islands, Jono?" Julie pleaded. "Please?"

I knew she was thinking about the story of the kids who ran away to an island and had a cow. I wondered about that. Would cows be moved over there by boat? Or would they put them on the plane? Boat seemed more logical, but I had this image in my head of a cow being winched down from a helicopter. But maybe that was just from a movie, for dramatic effect, you know. I'd say they use the boat all right when they're not making a movie.

She couldn't understand why I said no, we couldn't go to the islands. We'd stick out like a sore thumb, I said. Before we knew where we were, we'd be all over the evening news.

"Why would we?" she asked. "We look normal, don't we?" She looked down at herself, as if to check.

She hadn't a clue. Can you imagine, two kids from Dublin with rucksacks and no visible means of support wandering around Inis Meáin in the middle of February? Gimme a break.

"Ah, but we don't speak very good Irish," I said. "That'd be a dead giveaway."

She bought that all right. She gave a little shrug and staggered along with her rucksack. She was beginning to figure out that running away isn't all that it is cracked up to be. Maybe she was even starting to think I'd been right to resist the idea for so long. But of course she wouldn't admit that. We were here now anyway.

I wondered what would have happened if me and Granda had made it on to the train that day, where we'd have ended up. I couldn't imagine him sleeping in a wind shelter, but I suppose he would have had some money. Not like us.

We bought some food for our lunch in a supermarket. Julie wanted a chicken sandwich, but it was four euros, and I said for that we could buy a whole loaf of bread plus some ham and cheese. She sulked for a while because she wanted the chicken sandwich, but, hey, I was in charge of the money; she didn't have a choice.

We found a place to sit in Eyre Square near this mad fountain they have, and I was just making these very artistic sandwiches with the bread and ham and cheese when this drunk came up and started talking to us. Maybe he wasn't really a drunk, but he had a bottle in his hand, and the smell off him was terrible. I tried to ignore him, but he wouldn't go away. He made a big point of telling us about what an intellectual he was, and how nobody ever believed that, just because he was homeless.

In the end, I gave him a sandwich; I thought it would shut him up. I figured he'd have to close his mouth to eat it. But he kept talking even with the food in his mouth.

"So what makes you think you're an intellectual, then?" I said.

I shouldn't have asked. I should have gone on saying nothing.

"I've read Edward Sye-Eeed," he said. "And *Don Quixote*."

"Uh-huh?" I said, not sounding very impressed, because I wasn't.

"In Spanish," he said, as if that was the cherry on the cake. "I translated it actually, into a poem. In iambic pentameter."

"Great," I said sarcastically. "I'm very glad to hear it."

"And the *Inferno*," he said.

I rolled my eyes.

"That's a movie," Julie said. "It's about a fire."

"Na, it's a poem about fourteenth-century Florentine politics," he said.

Idiot. Everyone knows Florida hadn't even been discovered in the fourteenth century.

I couldn't wait to get away from him. He gave me the creeps. I was afraid I might turn into him, if we went on living like this on the streets. We'd start to smell soon, I thought. Maybe we should go back to Salthill and have a swim and wash our clothes in the sea. Not a very attractive prospect in an Irish winter, but if you start not washing, that's how you end up, and that was a worse thought than being cold and having salt-stiffened clothes.

I unpacked one of Gramma's banana cakes, and I gave him a hunk of it. Then I put away what was left of the bread and ham and cheese and I stood up and said firmly, "We have to go now."

His mouth was full of the banana cake and he spat crumbs everywhere, but he insisted on saying, "I'm your man if you want any intellectual conversation. You'll find me here any time, day or night."

"Yeah," I said. "See ya."

I grabbed Julie by the hand and we marched off.

"I'll tell you all about the Galapagos next time I see you," he shouted after us. "Your little girl would like that."

"Would I?" said Julie to me. "What's a galapago?"

"I think it was a battle in the First World War," I said. "I don't think you'd be very interested."

After that we found the public library. It was great, lovely and warm and loads of books, and nice friendly librarians. I asked one of them about your man Sye-Eeed – it should be spelled Said, I found out, which is a bit hard to get your head around – and she said she thought I wouldn't really like to read his stuff until I am older. I thought that probably meant it was full of sex and violence, but I didn't argue. I didn't want to be drawing attention.

We stayed as long as we dared, and then we went to the cathedral, where they had some big prayer thing going on, with all candles lighting and flowers everywhere; it was very nice and quite warm and it smelled of candle grease and incense and carnations. Wouldn't you hate to be a Protestant and have a church that smells of mould? Though in fairness, I was only ever in one, and maybe it was not typical. Maybe they have lovely ones too that smell of . . . oh, gardenias or lilacs or something. They haven't got incense anyway. I know that. That's a Catholic thing; it's one of the differences, that and the rosary.

"Let's stay here tonight," Julie whispered, which was exactly what I was thinking myself, so before the service was over we crept into a confession box and hid there, one on each side of the priest's compartment, and we listened as the people streamed down the aisle, talking in Galway voices, saying *musha* and *yerra*, like in a play. It was very strange.

I was terrified a priest would suddenly decide to hear confessions and we'd be discovered, but it didn't happen, and in the end, the people all went out, and the place fell silent, except for this ticking sound that the central heating pipes made.

And then the priest's door did open after all, but instead of a priest getting in, to hear confessions, one got *out*. I nearly passed out with the shock of it. I could hear the soles of his shoes on the marble floor. What was he doing? Checking his pockets for something or picking his teeth? I stayed frozen inside my confession box, kneeling down – there isn't any other way you can inhabit a confession box, especially not if you have a great big rucksack with you. Sitting is uncomfortable, and lying down is out of the question, unless you are about two feet tall.

How could this man have been sitting within centimetres of my face for several minutes and not heard me breathing? How come I hadn't heard *him* breathing? I imagined him sitting there with the two little shutters on either side of him closed, not realizing there was a boy on the other side of one of them, and a girl on the other side of the other one. Suppose I'd sneezed? Suppose I'd been chewing gum? He *must* have heard Julie breathing. She breathes with great gusto, if you know what I mean – as if she really enjoys it.

But he didn't appear to have noticed a thing. Maybe those shutters are soundproofed, or maybe he was deaf. Or asleep. He might have been asleep.

I heard a tiny cough then, coming from Julie's part of the confession box. It was so tiny I knew she had tried to muffle it, and I hoped the priest wouldn't hear it. I sat very still, breathing through my ears, and waited to see if he would open her door to check. I could hear his feet still scuffing the floor just outside the confession box.

Seconds passed, they felt like weeks, and then I heard the door of the priest's compartment shutting with the soft knock of wood on wood, and the priest's footsteps moved away up the aisle. A moment later, a far door opened and closed, and then silence fell.

I crept out of my hiding place and opened Julie's door. She had managed to crouch in the dark wardrobey space, with her knees drawn up to her nose.

"Hello?" she said softly. "Jono?"

"Yeah, it's me," I said. "Did you tell that priest all your sins?"

"Nah, I don't commit sins," she said, standing up and stepping out of the confession box.

"Pride is a sin," I said.

"I'm not proud," she said, quite sure of herself. "It was fluffy in there," she added, blowing her nose. "And it smelled like the inside of a cutlery drawer. The kind in a sideboard, where you keep the best silver."

"Right," I said, only half listening to her babbling, as I looked around. The church was very still and shadowy and it felt vast, but it wasn't quite dark, because there were still candles lighted, and a red lamp glowing at the altar, and it still had that heavenly kind of smell.

"How did you manage to keep quiet?" I asked her then. "You must have been like a mouse in there, when he didn't hear you."

"I fell asleep," she said with a giggle. "I didn't even snore, did I?"

"Not even," I said, my mind boggling at the thought of Julie asleep on the floor of the confessional and the priest asleep in his armchair just inches away from her. "You're a topper. Come on, let's get you to bed."

So we unpacked our sleeping bags and stretched out on a pew, toe to toe, and we both slept for hours and hours. The sleep of the blessed, I suppose you could call that.

chapter eight

"Would you think Mammy is worrying about us?" Julie asked the next day, as we were having our morning tea.

"Nah," I said. "I don't think so."

"But we are her children," said Julie. "She'd have to worry, Jonathan, wouldn't she? We should have left her a note, said we were running away but we would be fine and she's not to worry."

"There wouldn't have been any point in that, Julie," I said uneasily.

"Let's text her," she suggested.

I didn't want to do that. I didn't want to be handing clues to the police on a plate.

"I never thought of charging my phone in that cathedral," I said, banging my forehead with the heel of my hand. "It's all out of juice. What about yours?"

"Mine is lost," she admitted.

"You lost your phone?" I pretended to be surprised. "Where did you lose it?"

"Jonathan!" she said with a giggle. "You *know* the answer to that." She added, "It's-a stu-pid ques-tion," in a sing-songy voice.

Gramma always said that. If you knew where you'd lost it, she reasoned, then it wouldn't be lost, would it?

Julie turned her palms out flat and held them in front of her in the air like little seal flippers, and then she jiggled them up and down in unison rhythm. I know she gets that from watching cutesy kids on TV, but it made me laugh all the same.

Then she said, "OK, so in that case, let's send her a postcard."

Resourceful child, our Julie.

I couldn't think of a good argument against that, and she kept on nagging about it, so in the end I let her get one, but I said she couldn't have a card that mentioned Galway.

"Ah," she said, and she tapped the side of her nose to show she understood my devious thinking. "OK."

So she chose a Real Ireland one that showed a pub front. It could have been anywhere. Anywhere in Ireland, I mean, it couldn't have been anywhere else.

Julie wrote the card:

Dear Mam

dont worry were ~~alrite.~~ all right.

Love from your kidz

Under that, she signed her name, making the dot over the *i* in *Julie* a little heart. Then she gave it to me to sign too, and she put a row of kisses on the bottom, under our names. They looked like tiny stitches.

We went walking around after that, looking for the post office. We didn't find the main one, but we went into this sweet shop on a corner to get a Twix (because there are two fingers, one for each of us), and they had a little post office counter in there, and luckily there was a cat. I knew Julie would not be able to resist that, so I said I'd queue up and get the stamp and she could play with the cat. As soon as I saw she was fully absorbed, I ducked out of the queue. I used the few minutes to send another text to Annie. Some nonsense about football. She likes soccer. I don't. I really have to work at knowing the scores and all, so I can talk to her about it. It's mad, 'cos usually it's the girl that doesn't like soccer. She supports Liverpool for some reason, and Shamrock Rovers.

I put my phone away – it wasn't out of juice as I'd said to Julie, but it was running very low by now – and then I called over to her and made a big show of dropping the postcard in the postbox, but I hadn't written the address on it.

As we came out of the shop, a Garda car pulled up beside us and the door swung open before the car had even come to a stop. The driver stuck his head out of the door and called, "Jonathan! Is that you?"

I don't know how I managed it, but I never flinched at the sound of my name, just went on walking. Luckily I was holding Julie's hand, so I was able to give it a fierce squeeze to warn her not to give us away, and fair dues to her, she got the message immediately and she never as much as faltered, just went on skipping along beside me.

The guard came after us and tapped me on the shoulder. "Jonathan?" he said.

I turned around. "Hello, Guard," I said cheerfully. "Are you talking to *me*?"

"Ye-es," he said, his eyes searching mine.

"On'y I'm Paul," I said, and I tried to make my voice country, or at least not Dublin. "I doan't knoaw inny Jonithins."

The guard looked sideways at me, and then he squatted down to Julie.

This is it, I thought. She's sure to say the wrong thing, and we'll be caught. My heart was doing jigs and reels inside my chest, and my mouth was dry.

"Hiya, Julie," he said.

Julie stared at him for a moment, and then she looked up at me and said, "He thinks my name is Julie, Paul."

God, she was a star. She should be on the stage.

She looked back at the guard and gave a gurgly little laugh, like Shirley Temple, and said, "My name is Arabella O'Brien."

Arabella! I nearly choked.

"What happened to your face, Arabella?"

Julie put her hand slantways across her mouth and said, confidential-like, "It was in a fight."

The guard tried to hide a smile. He stood up and brushed his hands together.

"Sorry," he muttered. "I could have sworn . . ." Then he looked suspicious again. "Rucksacks?" he said. "It's not holiday time."

"School bags," I said, and rolled my eyes to show I was not a happy – I was going to say not a happy camper, but I suppose I mean not a happy schoolboy. I was delighted that I'd used Julie's school bag as a rucksack for her. It had these pen and pencil motifs on it, all very businesslike. My own rucksack was just ordinary, but lots of lads carry their school stuff in ordinary camping rucksacks if not in sports bags. "An' yeah, we're dead late," I added. "Long story."

"I see," said the guard, and for two awful seconds I thought he was going to ask to look in the rucksacks, but he didn't. Instead he turned back to his car and opened the door. Just before he got in, he said, as casually as anything, "Where do you go to school?"

The pavement seemed to fall away under my feet, like a down escalator. This was it. I'd walked us right into it.

I looked over the guard's head, over the top of his car, and I saw – I couldn't believe it – a school! It looked like a primary school – a low building with a freshly tarmacked yard where they'd painted hopscotch on it, and high iron railings.

So I pointed and said, "I'm just dropping Arabella into her school over there, and I go to Scoil Ehnnnnnnhhh."

I'd somehow remembered that a lot of the schools in Galway are Irish ones, with *Scoil* as part of their name. I met a lad from Galway last year, he told me that. And I gobbled the last word—the old Closed Mouth is great for that – so it might be nearly anything.

The guard screwed up his face, but he must have thought I said something close enough to a real Galway school, because he got into the car and closed the door.

"Right, so ye'd better get yeer skates on and hurry along,"

he said through the window, which was fully rolled down.

The car screeched away from the kerb and Julie and I crossed the street, towards the school. When we got to the school gate we didn't go in, though, we just kept on walking. After we'd gone about a hundred metres, Julie pulled on my hand like a bell pull. "Did you like my name?" she asked.

I looked down at her. "Where did you get it out of?" I asked.

"It's my teddy's name. Gramma called her that. Miss Arabella O'Brien. She christened her the day she gave her to me, when I was four."

"I didn't know teddies could be girls."

"Well of course they can. Where do you think the baby bears come from?"

I laughed. But I knew they were on to us. It was getting serious.

We went wandering around for ages that day, not knowing where we were going or why, looking for somewhere warm, but everywhere was crowded in the city, and there was no place we could mingle in and not be noticed. And the money was beginning to get pretty low too. I don't know where it went, but we were down to coins now.

I desperately needed to think, but I couldn't think and be with Julie. The two things don't go together. I did have one thought, though. I thought: this could be it, so let's just enjoy today, or what's left of it. Wouldn't you know it, as soon as you think you should be enjoying a day, it turns really horrible on you.

That's what happened. It started to rain. Just a fine mist at first, but it soaked our hair and shoulders, and I knew we couldn't last the night out of doors. Julie started to cry with cold and exhaustion. She wanted to go back to the cathedral to sleep again that night, but I said no, that would be pushing our luck. What I really meant was, the guards were onto us, that priest probably heard us after all.

I took her into a chipper and bought two singles of chips with the last of my money. It was lovely and warm in there, and we made the chips last as long as we could. When we finally had to leave the greasy comfort of the chipper, we stepped out into driving rain.

"We have to go to Daddy's house," Julie moaned. "We *have* to. That's why we came, Jonathan, isn't it? Why are we walking around all the time, when Daddy lives here?"

"Julie," I said, and I was tucking her hair in between her clothes and her back to keep it dry, "I don't think we'd be welcome there."

"I don't care about that," she said. "I'm cold. I just want to be inside."

My heart was heavy, but I knew it was over. I'd done what I could, but we weren't going to be able to live forever like babes in the woods. I had tried to fool myself, but part of me deep down must have known that it was impossible. Why else would we have come to this city, if not so that I could deliver Julie over to Da when the time came?

"Have you got his address?" I asked her. I was just playing for time.

"We could ask the guards where he lives," said Julie. "They'll know."

She was shivering and whimpering, and I put my arm around her.

"Don't be silly, Julie," I said. "Remember that guard this morning? They're looking for us. It'd be a bit of a giveaway if we waltzed into the station and asked them where Da lives."

She smiled. "Oh, yeah," she said. "But why are they looking for us? We're not *crinimals*."

"You're not allowed to run away from home, you know," I said.

"Is it against the law?"

"Not exactly."

"Is it a sin?"

"No, not that either, but they can't let kids run around the streets with no one to look after them. There are people whose job it is to make sure they – we – are safe."

"Oh, well then, that's good. Let's find them and tell them we need to be safe."

"Only, there's still the problem of your face," I said gently. "Your bruise, I mean."

"It's dark," she said. "They won't notice."

"Sure thing," I said, but I didn't offer to go looking for the social services. "Only, they're probably not at work now, those people. They'll be at home, cooking rashers for their children and watching the telly."

"Rashers!" she whined. "So what are we going to *do*?"

Reluctantly, I put my hand in my inside pocket and pulled out a piece of paper.

"As it happens, I have Da's address," I said. "I found it in Gramma's desk."

I moved under a street lamp to read the address. It was in a place called Knocknacarra. I knew vaguely where that was because I'd seen a sign for it, out Salthill way.

"Let's go," I said, and I took Julie's wet little hand in mine and off we went in the direction of Salthill.

We trudged along for ages in the icy rain, and I checked the address a few more times. The piece of paper was wet and the writing was smudgy, but I could still read it, and every time I looked it said the same thing. I don't know why I kept re-checking it.

We entered the estate, and we wandered around parks and lanes and avenues and gardens, and in the end we found the crescent we were looking for. It was easy to find the right house because there was a blue light flashing in the driveway, whirling round and round on top of a Garda car.

You took your time, I said to them in my own mind. *Three days to track us down.*

"See that house, Julie?" I said, bending down to her level.

She nodded.

"That's where Da lives. The guards are there, but that doesn't matter now, because we're not running away anymore, see?"

She raised both eyebrows, but she didn't argue.

"Now, listen, I can't go in with you. I don't think Da wants to see me, right? But you are cold and wet and hungry, and you need to go in there and Da will look after you, because you are his little girl. Right?"

She was listening, but she gave no indication.

"So, I want you to go up that drive now and knock on the door, and ask Da to mind you. I can't go in with you, Julie, but I'll be all right, and I'll send you a postcard in a few days. OK?"

Julie's little two-tone face was streaming with rainwater. Or tears. She looked up at me, and she whispered, "No, Jono. No. You have to come too."

"I can't, Julie," I said. "It's complicated. Don't do as I do. Do as I say. Right?"

She gave a little shadow of a laugh. "Gramma," she said.

"Yeah. She always gave good advice. Off with you now, and don't look back. I promise about the postcard."

She nodded and took a step towards the door.

She turned then and said, "Wait a minute. I have to give you something."

She wriggled her rucksack off her back and opened it.

"Here, you hold these," she said, thrusting handfuls of clothes, worn and clean all mixed up together, into my arms.

At last she came up with what she was looking for. It was a hardback book with an uninteresting red cover.

"What's this?" I asked.

"It's your book," she said. "'Member when you sent me to get a book and a teddy. Well, I got the teddy, right, 'cos you said, which was good, even though I don't *do* teddies anymore, 'cos that's where I got the name, right? An' I got one of your books instead, 'cos you're a better reader than me. Right?"

In the middle of it all, I had to smile. Either she was taking me off, sending me up, or she had picked up that "Right?" thing from me.

"Right," I agreed.

The book looked vaguely familiar, but at the same time not the kind of book I would be reading.

I opened it at the title page. "*The Merchant of Venice*," I read. "By William Shakespeare. This isn't mine," I said.

"Well, it was on your desk."

Then I remembered. Mr O'Connell had given it to me. Said we'd be starting it soon and I might like to take a look over it ahead of the posse. "Steal a march", was how he put it. He has this weird idea I'm good at English.

"Well, that's great, thanks, Julie," I said, and I leafed forward in the book to the first page of the play.

"'In sooth, I know not why I am so sad,'" I read.

Huh! I thought. I could give him a few reasons.

"Is it a good one?" Julie asked anxiously.

I looked at her wet little figure standing there in the rain, her hair streaming and her mouth open on a rosy space with a gappy fringe of white teeth.

"The best book in the world," I said.

"You're only saying that," she said with a squirm, but I could see she was delighted.

"No, it is, really it is," I said, and I kissed the top of her head. Wet lemons.

Then she heaved the sodden rucksack onto her back again, and she took a step towards the house.

"Don't look back," I whispered. "Just keep going. And remember, you don't know where I am. Right?"

She stopped in her tracks.

"Go on," I urged her, and she did.

I waited no more than a couple of seconds, just long enough to see the door opening and Julie disappearing into the square of light.

Then I turned and ran and ran and ran into the rain, which was driving down now like chips of ice. I had no idea what kind of reception she got. They'd have to take her in, I thought. They'd *have* to. She's only eight. And the *guards* are there.

Part
TWO
school
social
phone
Daniel
foster

chapter nine

"So that's your story, and you're sticking to it?"

Paudge Rooney stared into Jonathan Kinahan's eyes.

"No," said the boy.

Rooney sighed and licked his pencil.

"Hmmm, here we go again," he said, pulling his notebook towards him. "So what happened?"

"I already told you," said Jonathan.

"But you just said you wanted to change your story."

"I never."

"So that's your story, and you're sticking to it. That's what I said, and you said no."

"Yes."

"Yes you said no, or yes you are sticking to it?"

"Yes I said no."

"So you want to change your story?"

"No."

"Jesus Christ, boy!"

Rooney's meaty fist thudded on the table between them. Jonathan jumped.

"Easy, Paudge."

It was the voice of the young woman they had assigned to protect Jonathan's interests during the questioning. A solicitor, maybe, or a social worker. They'd probably said, but he hadn't been listening. He didn't care.

He turned to look at her now. She was dark and stocky, and her hair shone as it slipped forward when she spoke. She wore a ring on her middle finger, with a huge mauve stone.

"Is that real?" Jonathan asked, laying a finger on the stone.

"Well, it's not imaginary," she said with a smile. Her chin jutted a little, but you didn't notice that so much when she smiled.

"He's running rings around me, Kate," said Paudge, shaking his head.

"What I mean is . . ." said Jonathan, turning back to Rooney.

"Aha!" said Rooney, sitting up straight, all business.

"What I mean is, That's your story, and you're sticking to it means I'm lying, but I'm not lying."

"It doesn't mean you're lying."

"That's the implication," said Jonathan evenly.

"Holy mother of God!" said Rooney, and he pulled his hair – he had a good thatch of it, like straw – with both hands.

Oh, lordy me, I can't keep this up. I thought the third person might make it all seem more real somehow, but it's hard work writing about yourself as if you are not yourself. You can't tell about what you are thinking, and that's really the whole point, isn't it? That's one for Mr O'Connell. Must ask him what he makes of that, only of course I won't be seeing him again. Not now. That's kinda sad. I liked him. But I've gone beyond all that now.

What happens to you if you have gone beyond school at fourteen?

But I didn't think that at the time. At the time, I thought, When this is all over, life might go back to normal. Not that it ever was normal to start with. I mean, normal, without "back to".

Life could go normal, I thought, and I could worry about girls and acne and deodorant and, oh, going to Oxegen and hanging about in front of the Central Bank and all that stuff that is supposed to preoccupy you when you are a teenager. It all seemed very distant somehow, from where I was sitting that day talking to Paudge and Kate, but I suppose I could learn. I am not averse to any of it really (that's a Gramma word, as in *I wouldn't be averse to a slice of that cake, Jon*). But I'm not averse to it, especially not the girls part. Birds, as Keith Butler would say.

There's Annie, of course. I know I said she was my girlfriend, but that's wishful thinking. I don't think she fancies me really, she just likes me, which is totally different.

This Kate one, now, I thought, she's not my type.

I didn't know I had a type actually, but I suppose it's like what people say about art: I don't know much about it, but I know what I like. In this case, what I don't like, and that's this sort of duck shape, though I do remember thinking, I'd say she's sound, as a person, I mean. And anyway, she's, hey, *twice* my age for chrissake, what am I even thinking of, like she cares what I think of her. Does that make her old enough to be my mother?

That word *birds* to mean girls, where did it come from? Gramma used to go out of her tree (pun not intended, but I like it anyway) if anyone used that word, with that meaning. She couldn't *stand* it. There's much worse words, I told her, but she didn't care, she just went spare when she heard *birds*. And the laugh of it is, she was just like a little sparrow herself, only a colourful one.

That eejit Keith Butler, he was talking about some bird one day, boasting about how . . . well, it doesn't matter, boasting anyway, and someone said something about birds of a feather, or nesting or twittering or some damn thing about actual birds, as in garden birds, songbirds – they were being smart, like – and Turdface Butler, he thinks they don't understand what he is talking about, and he says, *No, no, not that kind of bird. I mean the two-legged variety.* God, I nearly pissed myself laughing.

Mind you, it would be good if you could breed a four-legged turkey, for the Christmas market.

I have never seen anyone to suit their name so well as that Paudge guy. But to be fair he didn't seem too bad, for a cop. I knew I was annoying the hell out of him, but he was not giving me grief, not really. He's like the sort of bloke you'd like to have refereeing your matches, I thought, if you played sport. If anyone ever picked you for a team. If anyone thought you would ever be any good at anything.

Though maybe he was just playing good cop until the bad cop came. But I don't think so.

"Right, then, Jonathan," said Paudge, who is, as you know, on the pudgy side, which makes his name kind of amusing. If you can't help smiling every time you think of someone's name, it's hard to really think badly of them. Even if they are interrogating you.

That was supposed to sound businesslike, that "Right, then, Jonathan," so I sat up and looked serious. I wanted Paudge to be on my side. No, that's not exactly it. What I wanted was for me to be on the same side as Paudge. Not quite the same thing.

"So would you like to explain to us how you got into this mess?" he said. "Start again. Pretend I lost you the last time."

He did lose me the last time, the stupid old fart.

But like I said, he seemed a decent skin in his way, so I started to make a stab at explaining myself again.

"Which part of the mess would you like cleared up first?" I asked in a jocular voice, to set the tone, to show I'm not afraid, to invite his friendship. And also because I was not sure where to start. Plus I was not sure how much he knew.

"Well, I think you could begin by explaining why you left the scene," he said.

"The scene? You make it sound like a film." I snorted, to show this was a joke. "Cops and robbers."

He was not amused.

"Well, I don't like to call it the *crime* scene, Jonathan," he said quietly, looking at me in this straight-talking, we're-guys-who-trust-each-other kind of way. "I don't want you to think I am jumping to any conclusions here."

"Crime?" I said, trying to sound surprised. I hoped there wasn't a wobble in my voice. I knew we had to get to this eventually, but that's a big word, you know?

"Incident," he amended.

That was more like it. I sat back in my chair and crossed one leg over the other.

He eyed me suspiciously. He didn't like it when I seemed to be comfortable. I said nothing for the longest time. Kept him waiting.

In the end, I said, "My grandmother died."

Everything changed.

I don't know why.

Paudge jumped up and leaned over the table so that his face was within kissing distance of mine. I didn't like that. His breath didn't smell so very marvellous, for one thing. Close up, his face was kind of mealy, and the pores in his nose were black.

"Leave your feckin' granny out of it," he wheezed. "It's not your granny we're interested in here."

Touchy, I thought. Or pretending to be?

You were right, Mr O'Connell. Not a good place to start. Nobody seems to understand about Gramma dying, how that's when it all went totally pear-shaped.

I never understood that expression. What's wrong with pear-shaped? If you're an apple or an orange, I suppose it would be bad, but for almost anything else in the world – frig it all, in the *universe* – what's wrong with pear-shaped? It's good for pears, and it's good for aubergines, for vases, for decanters, for lightbulbs . . .

"Paudge!" said Kate, and she pulled him back by the cuff of his shirt. "Let him tell it his own way."

"He's playing for time, Kate," said Paudge wearily. "We'll be here all night at this rate."

I nearly felt sorry for him, there. He's not naturally a patient type, I feel.

"Doesn't matter," said Kate. "We're not going anywhere."

Paudge sighed and sat back in his chair.

"Well, home would be nice," he muttered.

Yeah, I thought. Home would be fabulous actually.

"And before midnight would be smashing."

"Could we have some more comfortable chairs?" I asked.

The chairs were those black plastic ones with a long slit of a hole at the bottom, where the back meets the seat. When we were kids, once we were at a concert and they had these chairs, and Keith Butler said the hole was for farting through, because if you farted into that kind of rigid plastic, there would be an explosion, and for the whole concert

I kept trying to line my arse up with the hole in case I felt the need to fart. It didn't really work, but it was more interesting than the concert.

Paudge sighed an exasperated sigh. "No," he said. "If you don't like the chairs, you can tell us your story quickly and clearly and then maybe you can go somewhere where the furnishings are more to your taste."

"It was you I was thinking of," I said. I could see how the chair buckled every time he moved, straining to contain his fat backside.

"Don't worry about me. Tell me about your sister."

That was the first inkling I had that they'd been talking to someone else from my family. Probably my da.

"Her name is Julie," I said.

"Yes. We know that."

"She's eight years old and she hurts easy," I said.

"Jonathan," said Paudge between clenched teeth, "stoppit now."

"What?"

"You know."

"I don't know."

"OK," said Paudge, and he creaked back in his bending chair. "OK, we'll let that go for now. Go on."

I had no idea what had happened once I'd delivered Julie to Da's front door in Galway, but the cops were there anyway, and they'd obviously had a word with her. She's a great kid, but she doesn't really have all that much cop-on. (Another bloody pun. I'm feeling very punny tonight.) The Arabella O'Brien moment was just a fluke.

So I said, "I brought her to Da. I thought she'd be safer with him."

"Than with you," said Paudge, nodding.

"*No!*"

He looked up and raised his eyebrows. They were fair and bushy, like false eyebrows that you'd buy in a joke shop, only bleached.

"Well, yeah," I said, "but only because I couldn't look after her anymore. I'd run out of cash. And she was so cold, you know?"

"Ah, the cash," said Paudge. "Now that you mention it . . ."

"That's not important," I muttered.

"You think it's not important that you held up a petrol station and terrorized a poor young girl and got away with three hundred euros?"

OK, OK so I had done that. That was why the police had nobbled me – presumably. The Galway police, I mean. We were back in Dublin now. I think the lads in Galway didn't know what to make of me, so they put me in a squad car, and that's how I landed under the care of one Paudge Rooney.

"I didn't get away with it," I muttered. "And I didn't hold anyone up. I just told the girl to give me the money, and she did."

"You threatened her!"

"I did not. I just pointed a carrot at her."

As soon as the carrot came into it, Kate started to laugh, but she didn't want Paudge to notice, so she clamped her mouth tight and the laughter all came snorting down her nose like an avalanche. Her whole body went into spasm. Her boobs were bouncing off the table, where she'd rested them. I hadn't noticed her boobs that much before;

enormous they were, how could I have missed them?

Paudge turned to glare at her.

"Thanks, missus," he snapped at her.

Kate's boobs just went on bouncing on the table. I had to look away. I could feel my stomach muscles dancing with laughter under my belt, and I concentrated very hard on keeping a straight face. Hysteria, I suppose.

"I didn't hurt the young one," I said after a moment.

"No," conceded the guard, "you didn't actually physically hurt her. But the poor girl is in a terrible state. Post-traumatic stress syndrome. They sent a report up from Galway."

"That was nice of them," I said sarcastically. But I was thinking, That's what *soldiers* get that have been in a war. I couldn't imagine that even a very sensitive girl would take being held up with a carrot all that seriously. But I pulled a grave face for Paudge's sake. I didn't want him to think I was heartless. Which, by the way, I totally am not. Ideally, I would not have done it, but I was desperate. I mean, I knew they had video cameras and everything, I knew I'd probably get caught, but I still had to do it; I couldn't last another half hour without something to eat and without going somewhere warm.

"I'm sorry about the girl," I said, and I meant it. "I'll send her a card."

"You will *not*, you blackguard," said the guard, and the fist came down again on the table.

"Right, so," I said. "I won't."

"I think," said Kate, "it's time we all had a cup of tea."

She tapped the face of her watch and made some sort of a signal to Paudge, who sighed and shut his notebook.

chapter ten

You'd never think it would work. I didn't really think so myself. I did need the money, I was serious about getting it, but the carrot part was just a bit of a lark.

I'd been walking around all night in the rain after I'd dropped Julie, stopping in doorways, dodging cop cars, moving, moving, trying to keep awake, starving.

I thought morning would never come, though what good morning was going to do, I didn't know.

It did come in the end, of course, and the shops started opening up, and still I was walking, walking, no plans, no idea what I was going to do next.

I was passing this mad hip vegetable shop, see, where they had all these lovely shiny veggies out on the footpath – Galway's like that, thinks it's in the south of France or Sicily or some damn place. They were setting up for the day, and they were in and out with crates and boxes. As soon as the shopkeeper went back in for another box, I sidled by the half-set-up display on the pavement and I nicked this carrot, as you do, 'cos I was hungry. It was the only vegetable I could think of that I would want to eat raw. I never went in much for tomatoes. Flavourless watery old things.

I strode on around a corner and then I took two bites of my carrot – OK, the shop's carrot – and then I looked at it, and I thought, You could be a gun. I have no idea where that thought came from, but it tickled my fancy, so I stuck the carrot in my jacket pocket to see if I could make it work. I was passing a clothes shop with a mirror in the window. I took a look at myself, and I wiggled the carrot and said, "Stick 'em up!" in an American voice, like a gangster in the movies.

This little old man was going past with a stripy shopping bag and he jumped. Then he saw that I was watching myself in the mirror, play-acting, and he started to laugh.

"Musha, laddie," he said, "you had me near convinced. I was all set to give you my pension money."

He gave this chortle and he patted me on the shoulder as he went by, shaking his head.

"That's a good one," I could hear him saying to himself. I was imagining him going home to his wife and saying, "Com'ere till I tell you the good one that happened to me today, Mary."

Anyway, I thought to myself, if that ol' fella got a fright, it must be convincing enough, so why don't I try it out on someone who could hand over a wad of cash? I've always liked that expression, "a wad of cash". It sounds so *generous* somehow, the way you would have so much, you wouldn't be bothered even counting it, it'd just be a numberless *wad*.

The young one in the petrol station grinned at me when I asked her for the cash. I don't know whether she thought it was some sort of a practical joke, or whether she just knew fine well that the guards'd be all over me in two seconds, but she certainly didn't look very worried. I did get hold of the wad of cash, all right. It wasn't a huge amount, because it was still early in the day, but even twenty euros would have done me. I really just wanted some breakfast and maybe money for a pair of gloves. I nabbed a couple of Lunch Bars and a banana as I left the premises, but I'd only crossed the forecourt when this police car came wailing up and three of them jumped out, and before I knew it, there I was, talking to the lovely Paudge.

There I go again, going on as if things happened in jig time. There was a bit more to it than that. They took me into a local station first, and it was the following day before they sent me back up here to Dublin, when they worked out who I was.

That makes me sound famous. I could do without that kind of fame. I'd rather not be anybody in particular. I'd much rather never have had anything to do with the police.

chapter eleven

The tea was truly awful. I am not what you would call a connoisseur, but I have to say that anyone who puts in the milk while the teabag is still in the cup really does not know much about tea. There is a kind of grey that you just don't want to drink. And especially not out of polystyrene. Even when we were homeless, me and Julie, those few days in Galway, we got a decent cup of tea.

They gave me a Penguin bar, though, which nearly made up for the tea.

We all settled down again after the unsatisfactory tea break, and Paudge made a valiant effort to take hold of things.

Too valiant.

"Now, son," he said, inserting his large freckled hand between his fat thighs and pulling his plastic chair forward by the rim of the seat, "tell me, was it you that killed your mother?"

Jesus!

My hands started to TREMBLE.

"Paudge!" Kate's voice was like a bullet, but a bullet that had been shot somewhere very far away.

My fingertips were slithery with sweat.

My heart was pounding in my head.

Just as well I'd finished that lukewarm ditchwater they call tea or I'd have splashed it all over myself.

I looked

d down n

and I saw that my legs

were SHAKING too.

If I'd been standing up,
I'd have fallen down.

He'd changed his mind about not jumping to conclusions. Or else he was trying to shock me into some sort of admission.

I didn't answer. I just stared at him. I think I forgot to breathe.

In sooth, I know not why I am so sad.

Rooney didn't move. He just stared me down.

Ma, I kept thinking. Ma . . . Dead.

Oh, my sweet Christ, they found her, and she *was* dead. It had to be true, or he wouldn't have said so, would he?

I kept seeing her face and it would disintegrate before my eyes, and then reappear, reassemble itself, like a pixellated image. Her eyes were dull and her hair was lank and her mouth was open, as if to say, "Jono, son, why did you . . . ?"

I mean, yeah, she wasn't the best mother in the world, but, hey, you know, she was *my* mother. *You only have one mother.*

And as if it wasn't bad enough that she was dead, poor old sot, this fat fool thought I'd killed her.

"I think you might want to rephrase that, Guard,"

said Kate acidly.

She put a hand briefly on the back of my hand. That did it. That moment of contact. I felt a sob rising up and I put my arms out on the table in front of me and buried my head in them. I could smell the clean wool smell of my jumper sleeves – they gave me this jumper, because all my other clothes were in the wash. I kept my eyes closed, and the darkness was like a safe place where I didn't have to think. I could feel Kate's hand resting lightly on my back, between my shoulder blades. She patted a few times, but she didn't push it, you know, she didn't make a meal of it.

Eventually I raised my head.

Everything was midnight blue for a moment and gradually the room came back into focus as I looked at it.

I rested my elbows on the table and cupped my jaws in my hands, and I nodded at Paudge, to show I was ready to go on.

"Jonathan, do you want a break?" Kate whispered.

"We've just had tea," muttered Paudge, as if that was what breaks were for. Tea. Not for understanding that your mother was dead. And that you were suspected of being implicated in it.

I didn't trust myself to speak, but I gave a minimal shake of my head. I had to get through this, and there was no point in putting it off.

"Right, then," Paudge said. "Sorry, son."

At last I managed to unstick my tongue from the roof of my mouth, and I said, "Don't – call – me – that!"

She called me that, on good days.

"Oh, yeah, sorry . . . Jonathan," he said. "So, tell me about the night your mother died, then. Will that do you?" The question was directed at Kate, but he kept his eyes on me.

And I said, "I didn't know." My voice came out really tiny and squeaky, like a kid.

"What didn't you know? That we were onto you?"

"Paudge!"

We both ignored her.

"No! I mean, I didn't know she was . . ." I gulped. "Dead," I finished, in a whisper.

"You didn't know, yeah, for sure," he said sarcastically. Then he muttered something under his breath. I thought it was *You bloody did!* but I couldn't swear to it.

Kate's hand, the one with the big ring, appeared on his sleeve, and gave it a tug.

"All *right*!" he said, and then he turned to her and said in a whisper, "Listen, I know you have to watch out for him. I'm doing my best here, but this is *serious*. A woman is dead here, you know?"

She said, "Yes, and it's his mother. No matter what, that means something."

"Yeah," he said shortly. "Yeah, I know. I understand. But . . . I have a job to do here."

She said nothing. Didn't even nod.

He clammed up completely then, too.

There was silence for what seemed like a g e s.

My vision kept coming and going, black and then

in full colour, and then totally black again, as if my electrics were faulty.

I was still seeing Ma's face coming and going in front of my eyes, and hearing her moaning at me, "Why, Jono?"

I couldn't stand it. I jumped up from my seat and I said, "OK. She fell."

Rooney looked up and raised an eyebrow.

"She was drunk," I said, and I slapped my hand on the table in front of his fat, self-important bulk as I sat down again. "She was drunk, and she fell. But I didn't know she was dead."

"Did you push her, Jonathan?" Paudge asked, his voice a raspy whisper.

"Of course I didn't! What sort of a person do you take me for?"

He blinked. He didn't open his mouth, but that blink said it all. *The kind of person who holds up a young girl in a petrol station – and OK, so it was only a carrot, but how was she to know that?*

Even his eyelids were freckled, and his eyelashes were so fair they were almost invisible.

"Maybe you were angry with her. She wasn't exactly Mother Teresa, I believe."

"I was angry with her," I admitted.

"Understandable," he said quietly.

Good cop.

"But I didn't push her. She was my *mother*. I looked after her for *years*."

I felt a tear trickle down my face, and I rubbed at it with my sleeve. I didn't want to cry now, in front of this pig-man.

"I never touched her," I said, and my voice was hoarse because I was trying not to cry.

"Come on now, Jonathan," he said. "Are you sure about that?"

"I didn't touch her!" I stood up again and paced the room. "I never laid a hand on her. In fact . . . it was . . . she was the one who pushed *me*."

"Ah, come off it, Jonathan. You're just saying that to confuse matters, now. Why would she push you? She comes in drunk and she pushes you. It makes no sense."

"I . . . I had been asleep," I said.

"You were in bed? You're saying you'd gone to bed? So she pushed you out of bed? Is that it? She must have been really up for a fight if she woke you up to have it."

"No."

"So where were you sleeping then?"

I closed my eyes.

I'd been sitting on the sofa, after Julie'd gone to bed. Ma was out.

I was sitting there with Julie's phone in my hand, I'd just sent that text message to Pukeball Butler's pukey little sister, and I was puzzling over what to do and the thoughts were whirling in my head, like clothes in a washing machine. We were in the spin cycle now. Foster bruise. Social school. The sleeves were wrapping themselves round the collars, the washing ball had worked its way into a pocket, a glove fingered the toe of a sock.

Scum... School... alco...

social...

Danielle... foster...

bruise... phone...

cow...

"On the sofa. She woke me up, told me to go to bed."

"Gotabed. Itsallhours."

"So what did you do? You went to bed, did you?"

"I . . ."

"Jonathan, you're stalling. You're making it up as you go along, aren't you?"

My ears rang, my eyes opened, and I jerked awake. Ma was swaying in front of me. She was smiling maniacally.

"Sssbedtim," she slurred, like she was a proper mother, only drunk.

"No," I said. "I'm just trying to remember."

"Right," said Paudge. "And what do you remember?"

"But I thought, see . . ." I said to Paudge, "I thought *she* was the one who needed to go to bed, so I stood up and I took her arm, and . . ."

"You just said you never laid a hand on her," said Paudge sharply.

"That's because I didn't."

"But if you took her arm, Jonathan, as you've said just there now, then you did lay a hand on her."

"Forff . . . ' I started, but then I took a deep breath. "Yes," I said as patiently as I could, "but—"

"So you admit that you did lay a hand on her?"

"NO! I *admit* nothing! But if you want to be so bleedin' *literal* about it, yes, I did literally touch her. I took her by the elbow. I meant, I never laid a *violent* hand on her."

"That's not what you said."

"It's what I meant, and you bloody well know it, you bastard."

I shouldn't have called him that. It was bound to make him tetchy again.

"I know nothing of the sort," he snapped, "but go on."

"Well, I was trying to get her as far as the stairs, see, so she would go up and go to bed, but she didn't want to, and she lashed out at me. She hit me a wallop on the chest. I fell back."

"On to the sofa? You fell on to the sofa?"

"No-o, not exactly."

"On to the floor, then? Did you fall on the floor? Come on, tell me what happened. Or did you stand up to her for once in your life and hit her? Did you? I mean, that would have been understandable, wouldn't it, if you'd lashed out at her."

"No!"

"You didn't hit her?"

"I . . . I think I kind of staggered against the sofa, and then I lost my balance and I fell right back on to the floor."

"You think."

"I think."

"You're not sure?"

"No, not a hundred per cent."

"Why not?"

"Concussion," I said, with sudden relief. That was it. Concussion. "I . . . I think I must have banged my head – I had a lump like a tennis ball the next morning. I probably passed out."

"Probably?"

"Yeah, I must have, because I don't remember Ma falling."

"But she did fall?"

"She must have, because when I woke up she was lying there beside me. She must have pitched forward. Yeah, because she was lying half on her stomach, half on her side." There was a long silence.

"I'm not sure I believe that, Jonathan," said Paudge at last.

I looked up at him. "But it's the truth," I said. "That's what happened."

In sooth, I know not why I am so sad.

"You are saying that you never touched her?"

"As you said, I did literally touch her."

"But you did not push her or trip her or fight with her?"

"No."

"So what makes you think she fell, then?"

"Well, she hardly lay down on the floor beside me because she was sleepy."

"Or concerned about you?"

Huh!

"I suppose I stepped back when she pushed me, and that made her lose her footing. She would have fallen forward, wouldn't she?"

"You're sure of that, Jonathan? Think very carefully now, before you answer me."

"Sure of what? I'm not sure. I didn't see her fall, I had passed out."

"But you're sure you never touched her – except to try to move her to the stairs?"

"Yes."

"Right. I see." Rooney closed his notebook and then he closed his eyes. He rubbed them with his hairy fists, and then he opened them again and said, "Well, in that case, can you explain the fact that the forensics people found strands of your mother's hair in your room?"

What was he getting at *now*?

"Well, we lived in the same house," I said. "She came into my room sometimes, she was my *mother*. Sometimes she even brought me clean sheets."

She hadn't done that for about six months, but this fat fecker didn't need to know that.

He looked at his notebook.

"Yeah," he said, "in the sheets, that's where the hairs were."

My heart started to hammer. I could hear it in my head, like a highwayman coming pounding over the hills.

"What are you getting at?" I whispered. "What are you suggesting?"

"Nothing, Jonathan," he said. "I'm only asking. But, look, the report says the hairs had roots. We're not talking about hairs that just got shed. We're talking about hairs that got pulled out of her head. Now, that doesn't look so great, does it?"

I sat back in my chair and closed my eyes.

"Listen, Jonathan." I could hear his voice, even though my

eyes were closed. Wouldn't it be good if you could close your ears too? Earlids. "It looks as if there was a fight, and if there was, the best thing you can do would be to own up to it."

I went on leaning back in my chair, with my eyes still closed, and still I said nothing.

"If you had been scrapping with your mother," he droned on, "you might have pulled her hair, you know? And you might have had hairs of hers wound around your fingers. That'd explain it. Were you scrapping with her?"

I opened my eyes.

"Scrapping? With my *mother*? Of course I wasn't. Are you mad?"

Paudge sighed. "I'm not mad," he said. "I'm just telling you what the evidence is."

"Yeah, you said . . . in my bed!" I felt sick.

He said nothing.

I closed my eyes as tightly as I could and tried again to remember. I'd put all this out of my head, and now I had to make an effort to get hold of it.

"As I fell . . ." I said, opening my eyes again, "I think possibly I might have grabbed her hair."

"Right," said Paudge. "So you never laid a hand on her, but you did catch her by the elbow, and now it seems you also pulled her hair. I thought you said there was no question of a scrap."

"No!" I yelled at him. "I wouldn't hit my own mother, for the love of God. I pulled *at* her hair, I mean. Not that I pulled it."

"That's a very subtle distinction," said Paudge.

"What I mean is," I said, "that as I fell . . . I . . . well, maybe I clutched for something to hang on to, to stop myself from falling, the way you do when you're losing your balance."

"You mean, you pulled her down with you, right?"

"Wrong. If I grasped her hair – well, that could happen. Her hair is long, you know. Was." My voice broke on the last word, but I pulled myself together and continued. "I don't remember, but I did try – I mean, I think I would have tried . . . to reach for something to hang on to. So maybe I did grab her hair as I fell. It's natural to do that."

"Hmmm," said Paudge.

He read on for a moment, his lips moving silently.

Then he looked up. "Well," he said, "that's fair enough, I suppose."

I put my head in my hands.

Kate spoke then. "Jonathan," she said, "I believe you."

"You keep out of it," Paudge barked at her. "It's got nothing to do with you."

Kate didn't reply. She just swung on her chair and looked at him as if he was a very bad puppy who'd poohed on the floor.

I swung back in my chair too, and I kicked the leg of the table. I may even have smirked a little.

Then Rooney starts in at me again: "So maybe you didn't actually kill your mother, Jonathan. I hope that's true. But you left her to die, or you left her dead, and then you scarpered. Whatever way you look at it—"

"I left her to sleep it off!" I hissed. "I left her to sleep it off hundreds of times before. How was I to know that this time—"

"This time, she was conked out on the floor!" said Rooney.

True. But even so . . .

"She was snoring when I left the room," I said.

"Snoring? You never mentioned snoring before."

I ignored that part.

"Dead people don't snore," I said. Well, that was obvious, but I needed him to make that link. "And I put a blanket over her," I added. "What else was I supposed to do?"

"Call an ambulance?" he suggested.

"Just a minute," I said, straightening up in my chair and staring into his face. "Your hypothesis . . ."

He looked startled at that word. Maybe he didn't understand it. That's a bit mean of me. OK, maybe he just didn't expect me to know it.

"Your hypothesis is that I'm lying, right? You think she was dead already. That I made the snoring up?"

"Maybe."

"So now you want me to call an ambulance for a dead person? Well, you know what, they don't do resurrection at any hospital around where I live. So why would I call an ambulance if she was dead?"

Oh, God. I'd walked right into that one. I was arguing the wrong case.

Now it was Paudge who smirked.

"Exactly," he said. "If I'm right, you didn't call an ambulance because she was already dead, and you knew it. You just left her there and you scarpered."

"No. The reason I didn't call an ambulance was that I never called an ambulance for her, not once in all the years since Da left, and on every other occasion that I didn't call an ambulance for her, she woke up the following morning. Or afternoon. If I called an ambulance every time she passed out drunk—"

"Except that this time," he said, "(a) she was dead and (b) you left altogether. That's a bit of a coincidence, isn't it?"

"No."

"It's not a coincidence? No, it's not. You left because you knew she was dead. Right?"

"I mean, yes. It's a coincidence."

"Well, which is it? A coincidence or not a coincidence?"

I was confused. "How was I to know . . . ?"

"You didn't think to look in on her in the morning, to see that she was all right?"

What? My confusion lifted and anger raced through my veins. How come *I* was supposed to be responsible for *her*?

"I *never* looked in on her in the mornings. I waited for her to surface."

What the hell did he know? All the times I'd put her to bed, taken her shoes off, made sure she had a glass of water and a basin for puking into. All the times I'd cleaned up her messes. All the times I'd covered for her. Ringing her up on dole day.

"Bitch," I muttered. (I'm not proud of that. I was under pressure.)

"You left her to *rot*," he said.

I gasped. That was carrying literalism a bit too far.

"For God's sake, Paudge, ease up," said Kate. "You're bullying him."

You stupid old wagon, Ma, what did you need to go and die for?

My chest was heaving with suppressed sobs.

Paudge said nothing for a while. After a few minutes he said, "Right. We'll leave it there for now. Would you like something to eat, Jonathan?"

Food? My stomach was clenching with sobs, but even so, it did a little flip of excitement at the thought of food. Apart from the Penguin bar, I hadn't eaten for hours.

I blew my nose.

"Not if it is any relation to the tea I got earlier," I said. I have some self-respect.

"Always the bitter word," Paudge said. "But no. We could go to Max Snacks if you like."

He could do bad cop, good cop all by himself, this one.

"You're joking!" I said, and suddenly I felt I was going to

cry. I've never found the thought of hamburgers moving before, but for some reason, at that point it seemed like the kindest treat, and I was overwhelmed by it.

"No," he said, hitching up his belt as he stood up from his chair. "I think we can rise to an oul' hamburger. If you're interested."

That is how I found myself eating a double-decker and chips in a brightly lit yellow-furnished cube of glass with a fat plod and a nice lady with a bad figure, and with unshed tears pricking at my eyelids.

Christ, it's a long, long way from there to here.

chapter twelve

They'd found a place for me in some kind of home for delinquents, they told me over the Big Burgers. They didn't use that word, but I knew what they meant. It's just outside Dublin, lots of fresh air, they said. I was never a big one for the fresh air, and frankly I'd got more than enough of it over those few days in Galway to last me a lifetime. I'll be crippled with arthritis by the time I'm fifty after all the soakings I got.

Gramma always said she felt sorry for delinquents. She said, *I bet they've had a horrible life. I bet something went terrible wrong in their family.*

I never thought I would be one myself.

It was the carrot job that did it. I don't really think they can be serious about me killing Ma, but they'll have no trouble nailing me for the carrot.

It's kind of weird, but even when you know someone is dead, you sometimes have this sort of conviction that it hasn't really happened, and if you do the right thing then they will somehow be undead, and it'll all come right. The only problem is to know what that right thing is.

I was still in that phase. I suppose it's shock or something. I had this mad sort of idea that if I behaved myself properly with this Paudge, then it'd be OK, Ma wouldn't be dead after all. It bothered me, though, that I'd done the carrot job. I had this eerie feeling that this was at the nub of the problem.

Paudge had me worried there for a while, about the hairs. I was even beginning to think myself that maybe I'd done it. By accident. But I didn't. I want you to believe that.

I finished my hamburger and licked my fingers. Then I wiped them with the little piece of tissue they give you, and I wiped my mouth too. I folded the tissue up and tucked it into the cardboard box they put those stupid skinny chips in.

"All right," I said, meaning about what they were calling my *placement*, as if I was a chess piece that they had found a perfect move for. The fight had gone out of me.

"Can I see Julie soon?" I asked.

Paudge looked at Kate. Evidently she was the one they had decided was going to do the dirty work.

"Not just for the moment, Jonathan," she said softly. "But

she's OK. She's well, and she's safe. You don't need to worry about her."

"Why can't I see her?" I asked. "Is it my da? Is he the problem?"

They didn't answer.

"Well, look," I said. "Tell yous what. You ask Julie if she'd like to see me, and you'll see. Her and me . . . well, I'll put it like this, we're very good mates. Look, she brought this book for me to read," and I pulled *The Merchant of Venice* from my rucksack. "We were running away from home, right, and *she* thought I might just like a spot of *Shakespeare* to keep me entertained. She's a howl, she is."

"Have you read it?" Kate asked. She was changing the subject, I knew.

"Of course I haven't read it," I said. "I don't speak Shakespeare. That's the whole point. That's why it's such a hoot that she brought it."

"It's a good story. You might like it."

Dream on. I didn't actually say it, but I raised my eyebrows so she knew what I meant.

These social worker types, like teachers, they are. Think they can save you with Shakespeare. It's kind of sad, really. They can't know much about reality.

chapter thirteen

***Antonio:** In sooth, I know not why I am so sad;*
It wearies me; you say it wearies you;
But how I caught it, found it, or came by it,
What stuff 'tis made of, whereof it is born,
I am to learn.

Yeah, well, it's the only book I've *got*, right?

So, good for old Antonio. He's sad and he doesn't know why. That's a bit of a luxury, that kind of sadness, if you ask me – and even if you don't. It has no cause. It's just a kind of *mood*. Maybe he was a teenager. I doubt if his grandmother has died, his mother has managed to annihilate herself, his father has run off with a young one, he's not allowed to see his little sister, and he's in danger of getting a criminal record because of a kind of overambitious prank with a carrot, or possibly for murder.

I'd give him sad, I would, if I met him.

Oh, sweet Jesus, is it ever going to let up?

I told Kate all that the next afternoon, when I saw her. She said, Yeah, you're right, I never liked Antonio, bit of a moaner. Spoilt.

I like her attitude.

All the same.

"What about that Paudge?" I said. "He's trying to get you to winkle stuff out of me, isn't he? That's why you're here."

"It is not," she said. "Listen, Jonathan, I am on your side. I don't owe Paudge anything. Don't get me wrong, I think he's OK, it's just . . ."

"I liked him, too, until he started accusing me of murder," I said. "You'd be amazed how a little thing like that changes the way you feel about a person."

Kate threw back her head and gave this long laugh. Her throat was all exposed and creamy. There's something very *healthy* about this person. I can't put my finger on it.

"Jonathan, your sense of humour will save you."

"Oh?" I said. "Not Shakespeare?"

"Shakespeare's dead," she said, "like a lot of people in your story. Now, listen. First off, I want to say, I am very sorry about your mam."

The lights started going on and off in my head again.

"Don't!" I said. "Don't call her that. That's what I called her when I was a little boy. I don't want to think about that."

Mam, Mam, help! I'm falling! I'm falling, Mam!

That was me, on my first bicycle, terrified. Ma was running along beside me, shouting, "You're all right, you're all right, keep looking ahead, concentrate, pedal, Jonathan, *pedal.* If you keep pedalling, you won't fall off. Pedal like crazy, Jono, pedal, pedal, pedal!"

But I kept looking back, to check that she was still holding on to the saddle, and every time I turned my head I lost my balance and she righted the handlebars with her other hand, and she screamed, "Don't, Jonathan. Just look ahead and pedal like the bejaysus."

But I didn't trust her, and in the end, one of my twistings-around knocked me so far off my centre of gravity that I came down with a bang. I hurt the side of my face, I scraped my shins, and I caught my foot in the spokes and sprained a toe. I sat there crying in the middle of the bicycle – it seemed to be lying all around me – and I yelled at her, "It's all your fault, it's all your fault."

She pulled the bicycle up and wheeled it away. She left me in a huddled heap, crying and shouting and hurting.

"I couldn't stand the noise," she explained afterwards. "I couldn't take the yells and shouts. And you were blaming me, it wasn't fair."

Of course it wasn't fair. But I was bloody six years old.

"Sorry," said Kate, about using that word, *mam*. "I won't. What I want to say is, I know this is very tough for you, but we have to face up to it all if we are to make any progress here. OK? You with me?"

God, she was going all social-workery again on me. But what choice did I have? She was the only person I could talk to.

I looked out the window. There was some kind of a five-a-side thing going on in the garden. And on the windowsill was this blade I'd found in a cabinet in the bathroom of that hamburger place we'd gone to, me and Kate and Paudge. God knows how it got there. It was weird, finding a thing like that, so weird, I had to take it. It was like a gift, I thought. So I'd wrapped it up in toilet paper, layers and layers, and I'd put it in my pocket and then I'd walked very stiffly for the rest of the day, in case it worked its way out of the toilet paper and started to do damage.

Once I got it here, I put it on the windowsill in the sitting room, just at the end, where it was hidden by the curtains. I wasn't so stupid as to put it in my own room. Nobody had noticed it was there. It made me feel sort of powerful or something. And then of course when I'd looked, two of my fingertips were scored and had tiny arcs of red. When I saw that, they started to sting.

"I have to see Julie," I said then. "Why won't they let me see her? Where is she anyway? Is she still in Galway? Still with Da?"

"No," said Kate. "He . . . eh, well, he turned her over to the social services."

"What!" My mouth was dry, my heart was pounding in my ears. After all the trouble I'd gone to to make sure Julie wouldn't get taken into care! Handing her over to bloody Da, the last person in the world I'd want to have her – second last, I mean.

"The social services, you know? We look after kids if their families can't."

"But Da is her family, and he can. That's why . . ."

Kate shook her head. "He doesn't see it that way," she said. "He thinks . . . well, he says she's not his daughter, and he couldn't be responsible for her."

"Not his daughter? What's that supposed to mean?"

"I couldn't tell you, Jonathan. Maybe he thought your mother . . ."

"But he adored Julie," I said. "He worshipped the ground she stood on."

"He walked out on her all the same," she said.

"So – where is Julie now?"

"We found a foster family for her."

Julie in a foster family. Me not able to see her. How the hell had I let it happen? I covered my face. I didn't want Kate to see what was in my eyes.

"It's here in Dublin," she was saying, "and it's not far from where you both live . . . eh . . . lived. She can go to the same school, which is good."

"She hated that school." My voice sounded like a mouse you'd squeezed under a door. "They bullied her."

I thought she'd ignore that, but she didn't. She wrote it down. "Right. We'll look into that, Jonathan, definitely. See if we can flush that out, but continuity is always good, you know."

"What about me? I'm continuity, I'm the best continuity she's got! She needs to be with me," I said.

"Well . . ." said Kate, "yes, but – you're not an adult, Jonathan, and . . . well, you're *here*."

She looked around her. It's nice, this place. There's a flat-screen telly, and my mobile was sitting on a coffee table, charging. I was planning to phone Annie later. I hadn't been able to charge my phone for days.

But I saw her point. I couldn't bring Julie here. It wasn't a place for little kids.

"They're lovely people, I promise you that," she said. "They've fostered lots of children. She will be happy there."

"Happy! She doesn't need a foster family. She's got me."

"I don't mean happy in that sense. I just mean she will settle, in time."

"In time! You can't be planning to *leave* her there! This is just a temporary arrangement, isn't it, until the guards have finished questioning me. Then I can go home, right?"

My heart was in my mouth. I could hardly bring myself to go on asking questions, in case the answer was unbearable. But not to know was even more unbearable.

"I could move?" I said again. "Back home? When this is all over, this nonsense about Ma. You know I didn't do it. She just fell over."

"Come on, Jonathan, tell me the story."

I shuffled my feet. I didn't want to talk about "the story". I wanted to talk about Julie.

"Why do you want to know?" I asked.

"I don't really want to *know*," she said. "It's more that I think it would be good for you to *tell* me."

I considered this for a while. It was a fine line, but I think I got it.

"I've told you," I said. "You heard me telling Paudge."

"What you said to Paudge doesn't count. I want to hear the whole story, your way."

I sighed again. "My grandmother died," I said.

I watched her face.

She nodded. "Uh-huh?" she said.

She didn't say it was the wrong place to start.

And so I told her what had gone on since Gramma died, and about the apples and the bruise and mitching off school and then how we'd left and all that went on, up to the moment I left Julie outside Da's house, and I ran off into the cold, wet night.

When I finished, my throat was sore from talking, and my jaw was clicking with exhaustion. Kate was biting her lips.

"God," she whispered, "you poor kid!"

I looked at her and I shrugged.

"So that's why you ran away, because you couldn't cover up about Julie any longer?"

"Yeah, mostly," I said.

"Nothing to do with your mother not waking up one morning?"

And that finally started me off crying. I stuck my knuckles into the corners of my eyes, but I couldn't stop the tears.

"In sooth, I know not why I am so sad," I said, when I'd had a good weep and was wiping my eyes.

"I could make a stab at it," she said. She was wiping her own eyes.

"OK," she said then. "Tear-fest over."

"Julie?" I said.

She must have heard the desperation in my voice, because she patted the back of my hand and said, "Tomorrow, Jonathan. I'll be talking to some people, your case will be up for discussion, and I give you my word of honour that I will do my level best to . . . well, to make sure you're both looked after in the best possible way."

What was *that* supposed to mean? Sweet feck all, as far as I could see.

"There's only one possible way," I said. "She belongs to me – with me, I mean. I brought her *up* – well, me and my gramma, we did it together. I am the only one who . . . They can't take her away from me. She *needs* me."

Then an awful thought struck me. "Is it because I gave her over to Da? Is that why they think I can't look after her, that I don't want to? I thought . . . I mean, I did it for the best. I thought she'd be better off. I didn't *want* to, but I thought he loved her."

"That was the bravest thing, Jonathan," she said very softly.

I looked up at her. I was sorry I'd thought those things about her looking like a duck.

"Yeah," I said.

I wanted to howl. But I just sat with my head down. I suppose you could say I'm not really a howler.

She said, "Tomorrow, Jonathan. I'll see you tomorrow."

chapter fourteen

We went on this holiday when Julie was a baby.

This particular holiday was different because we went to France, and we hired a car at the airport and drove off to this really cool campsite place with a pool and a place for barbecues and entertainment for the little kids and everything. It was a great holiday. There was soccer in the afternoons for the older kids, like me. Julie used to come and watch. She was only a toddler, but she sat patiently on the sideline and pointed at me every time anyone came by. I used to like soccer in those days, before I discovered I was no good at it.

I never remember Ma and Da so happy. There were babysitters, so they could go out in the evenings. When I say a campsite, we weren't in a tent, more a kind of mobile home. Only it wasn't mobile, it was up on bricks. I don't know why they call it mobile when it is immobile. Anyway, the babysitters would come and sit in the tiny living room and watch TV and Julie and I could stay up as late as we wanted to, and Ma and Da would go to the nearest town to one of the restaurants and eat fish. They never ate fish at home, but they said this was different. Maybe foreign fish taste better, I dunno.

We didn't speak any French, and the people running the campsite had desperate English. They thought they spoke English. They opened their mouths and these sounds came out, but they had nothing to do with any English words I ever heard. They would wave their arms a lot, though, and we more or less got the gist of what they wanted to say, because after all, what does a campsite person want to say except park your car over there or there won't be any hot water for showers until after six, and really, you can either work that out, or you can manage without knowing it.

The pool was really great. There was a small pool for the little kiddies like Julie, where they could waddle around in their nappies and splash their feet. And there was the shallow end of the big pool where the older kids could swim, and the parents used the deep end. They looked weird with their swimming caps on. You couldn't recognize people at all; they didn't look like themselves. One day I was watching Ma and Da swimming and splashing each other and roaring with laughter and then Da got out of the pool, and it wasn't Da at all, it was some bloke from Wexford that Ma and Da had met in the supermarket a day or two before.

On the last day of the holidays, we packed up the car with all the luggage to drive back to the airport, but our flight wasn't until evening, so we thought we'd have a last swim before leaving. Da had all the stuff for the airport in this little waterproof bag, like a toilet bag or something, the passports and the tickets and so on. Ma told him to put the car keys in there too, so all the important things would be in the same place.

Da put the little bag down on the ground beside this sun-lounger he was lolling on. Every two minutes, he shook the contents of the bag out as if to check something; it made him nervous having it all together and no place to keep it, as the mobile home had been handed over to the campsite people to clean it for the new family.

Anyway, we all had a swim, and then we had a picnic by the pool, and we got dressed behind the car for going to the airport. All except Da. He was still in his swimsuit. He didn't want to leave.

Ma said, "I wish you had left the car doors open, hon, it'll be like an oven in there – the children will roast."

"Nag, nag," said Da, gulping back a can of something fizzy. "We can open the windows as we drive. It will cool down fast."

Ma shrugged and went on pulling up Julie's socks. When she had the baby ready, she put her hand out and said to Da, "OK, gimme the keys, and I'll strap this one into her car seat while you get dressed."

Da leaned over and picked up the waterproof bag. He shook out the passports and the tickets on to the ground. Then he shook it again. No keys.

"Jono!" he yelled. "Did you take the keys out of this bag?"

I knew he hadn't put the keys in the bag. I'd heard Ma telling him to put the keys with the other things, but he'd just waved at her in that yeah-yeah-I-hear-you kind of way, and he never did it. But now, he'd obviously forgotten.

I couldn't say that. I couldn't remind him that he hadn't done what Ma said. That was the thing about Da. He couldn't ever just laugh it off if he made a mistake and look goofy. If you mentioned a mistake he'd made, he went ape-shit, so for a moment I just froze.

"Jonathan?" he said, in this piercing way he had when he was annoyed. If there was one thing worse than contradicting Da, it was ignoring him. I had to say something, so I said the first thing that came into my head.

"Why would I do that?" I said.

It was just an innocent remark, but Da was obviously in a tizzy about losing the keys, because he took it as some sort of a provocation, and he flew into a rage and he went for me with both his fists up.

Ma jumped in front of me, to stop him. She had Julie in her arms still.

"Put that child *down*!" Da roared at her. I think he thought she was deliberately using Julie as a shield.

Ma was paralysed. I could see that she just couldn't move, she was so scared, but Da thought she was defying him, and that ratcheted his anger up another notch, and he went ballistic. He got red in the face, he started foaming at the mouth, and he flailed out and hit everyone, me, Ma, even Julie. We went reeling back against the car, which was roasting in the sun. I screamed, not because of the blow, but because my arms got burned on the hot metal.

Everyone came running, all the French people who owned the place, and there was this huge ruckus and two of the French people knocked Da down and sat on him till the police came.

We missed our flight.

I don't remember what happened about the keys, but we must have found them in the end, because we drove off after the police had finished with Da. We had to stay in the airport overnight, and the bloke from Wexford turned up and he bought Ma a bottle of wine and she drank the whole thing herself, and Da was yelling at her and Julie was wailing crying all the time, and Ma was pissed out of her head and Da had a fight with the bloke from Wexford.

That was the first time I remember Ma drinking. She always drank, but I mean, serious drinking. And Da actually shook Julie to try to make her stop screaming, because everyone in the airport was gawping at us, but of course that only made Julie worse.

That's where I should have started the story. That was the beginning. But I'd forgotten that until now. I thought Da had never hit us, apart from the odd crack with the back of his hand, I mean, but it's amazing what you can forget.

It didn't explain about Da not wanting Julie, though. It couldn't have been the bloke from Wexford, because Julie was more than a year old by then. I suppose there could have been a bloke from somewhere else that I don't remember about.

Not that it matters. What matters is that I have to get Julie back.

chapter fifteen

I was desperate to see Julie. I kept asking them, every day, when could I see her. It was driving me crazy the way they kept us apart. We'd been together for eight years, and then suddenly we weren't allowed to see each other. It made no sense. She's my sister. I've looked after her all her life. And she has no one else. Da won't have her, and everyone else is dead. She needs me. I kept telling them that she needs me, but they didn't seem to see that.

Kate did her best, I know. She understands, but nobody else has the first clue. They're all control freaks, bloody jailers, they are.

They don't know about my friendly little razor blade on the windowsill. It's still there. I'd sack the cleaner if I ran this place.

In the end, they said we could go to the funeral, Julie and me. Nice of them, that. Big deal.

But I didn't say any of this, because I was so relieved that I was going to see Julie at last. I hadn't seen her for a week.

They brought me to this place, some kind of hotel, I think, and I was sitting in this big, deep leather sofa, and I remember thinking, This is a really cool leather sofa, and I wish I could appreciate it. But of course I couldn't.

Then the revolving door started to revolve, and I saw Julie trapped for a moment in that capsule of glass, her big blue eyes wide open, her teddy firmly pressed under her arm. That made me smile. She's supposed to be too big for teddies.

She was wearing clothes I'd never seen before, some kind of a pink top and pink tights and a little flowery cardigan and a grey corduroy skirt, and these cute little grey shoes with smiley faces on the buckles. She looked like just any little girl, not a kid who'd been wrenched away from everything she has ever known. Except for the bruise on her face. It was much better. It seemed to have shrunk, and it was yellowy green now, and not nearly so dramatic, but it wasn't going to just disappear for a while yet.

I jumped up and waited for the door to revolve another quarter circle, and then there she was, in front of me.

I hunkered down and said, "Hello, you."

She put up her arms and the teddy fell on the floor, but she stepped right over it and threw herself at me. I hugged her nearly to death. I practically ate her.

At last I let her go, and I picked up the teddy.

"Who's this?" I said. "A new one?"

"Daddy's new girl threw my Arabella O'Brien in the bin," she said. "They told me this one is nicer, but I preferred Arabella."

"So what is this one called?"

"Jonathan," she whispered.

"That's a nice name," I said, and she grinned.

"I hope you've changed your mind," I said.

"What do you mean?" She cocked her head on one side and looked up into my face, screwing up her eyes.

"I hope you prefer Jonathan to manky old Arabella."

A slow smile dawned across her face. "You mean *this* Jonathan," she said, poking a finger into my chest, "but you're pretending you mean *that* Jonathan." And she pointed at the teddy.

She's better at getting things these days. Growing up.

"That's right," I said. "How've you been? Are they minding you properly?"

She nodded. "Mam's dead," she said.

"So I hear," I said. "Does that make you sad?"

She considered for a moment, but she didn't answer. Instead, she asked, "Do you think she got our postcard?"

I thought of Julie's neat row of kisses along the bottom of the card and something in my chest constricted, but I said, "Oh, yeah, for sure."

She nodded at that, pleased, and then she asked, "So are we orphans now, Jonathan?"

I didn't know what to say to that. I couldn't say *Technically, no*, so I just shrugged.

"You didn't hit it off with Da?" I asked.

"It's his new girl," she said. "She won't let him be nice to me. She's only three, but he likes her better."

"I see," I said.

"When are we going home?" she asked.

I couldn't answer her. I looked at Kate, and she said, "We have to go to the church now, Julie."

The funeral was terrible. There was hardly anyone there, just us and the priest and Kate and the woman who came with Julie. She introduced herself as Julie's foster mother and said her name was Jean. She looked all right, but she's just a woman in a red coat. A stranger.

Kate said afterwards that was wrong, there had been quite a lot of people there, neighbours and so on, but if there were, they didn't come to talk to me. Maybe they were embarrassed. People are always embarrassed to sympathize with kids, I've noticed that. And this was not an ordinary kind of situation, so I suppose you can't blame people really. But it would have been nice to see a few familiar faces. It was very bleak, with the coffin blocking the aisle of the church, and a brass crucifix on it with Ma's name under it, engraved.

I kept thinking about the last time I'd seen her, stretched out, drunk and snoring beside a pool of vomit. They'd asked me if I wanted to see her before they put the lid on the coffin, but I said no, I couldn't bear to see her all waxy and dickied up by the undertakers, but now I was kind of sorry I hadn't, because I kept imagining her turned on her side and snoring softly under the wooden lid. I said that afterwards to Kate, and she said that image would disappear over time, and I'd remember her as she had been in life. I sure as hell hope that's true, because I definitely do not want to be haunted by that image.

We followed the coffin down the aisle, me and Julie in front, Jean and Kate behind. Jean was carrying the other Jonathan. There was some sad music on the organ, terrible shit it was.

I was concentrating on holding on to Julie and walking in time to the music, even though it was fierce music. This was the last thing I could do for Ma, and I wanted to do it right. But for some reason – I must have caught sight of her out of the corner of my eye, or heard something, I don't know – I looked to the side, and there was Annie, standing there in a pew watching me. Jamie was with her. We weren't the only ones after all.

I wanted to rush into the pew and bury my face in her hair. But I just raised my hand. Not exactly a wave, more a kind of signal.

They said we didn't have to go to the crematorium if we didn't want to, so we said we didn't want to.

I grabbed Annie outside the church and I mumbled

something in her ear, I don't know what, and she just kept squeezing my hand. "I'll phone you," I said, and I squeezed her hand back. "I'm sorry . . ."

She nodded, and then I got into the car with the others. They were taking us to some other hotel for lunch. I looked out the back window of the car, looking at Annie. She was standing there in her best coat, looking very thin and miserable, not a bit like my bouncy, funny Annie at all. You'd think she was the one whose mother had died instead of me.

After lunch, they told Julie she would have to go back to her foster home with Jean, and her lip started to tremble, so to distract her I gave her back her phone. I'd had it all along.

She was thrilled. "Where did you find it? I looked everywhere."

"That's for me to know," I said, "and you to find out." One of Gramma's most irritating sayings, but I understood now why she used it. Very handy way of ducking out of answering a difficult question.

Then they told her I couldn't go with her to Jean's, that I had to stay in my own place. She started to cry. I couldn't bear it. I wanted to die.

"Why?" she kept wailing. "Why?"

Well, they couldn't tell her why, could they? They couldn't tell her that I was officially considered a danger to her.

"Tell me about the bruise on your sister's face," Paudge had asked.

So I'd explained about the apples for dinner and Julie crying and Ma losing it, and how I'd kept her home from school for days, hoping it would heal up, and then when it didn't, how we'd made a break for it.

Paudge kept staring at me.

"That's exactly what you said before," he said.

I had told him all this already, in one of those endless, pointless conversations we'd had.

"Yes," I said. "That's because that's what happened. It hasn't changed."

"You're sure you aren't the one who hit her, Jonathan?" he asked quietly.

I saw red. Really, a red cloud came down over my vision and I started to kick and scream. My chest hurt, I screamed so hard.

"See?" he said, after I'd calmed down. "You seem to have a problem controlling your anger."

Like father, like son, I could hear him thinking. Although that made no sense, because I hadn't told him much about Da at all.

"I have *not*!" I shouted. "I only screamed and kicked the furniture. I didn't hit anyone, did I? I never hit people. I'm a sap. I wouldn't hurt a fly. And certainly not an eight-year-old girl."

"No?" he said. "Not even Danielle Butler?"

"*What*? What are you on about? What has Danielle Butler got to do with anything?"

"Danielle Butler got an extremely threatening and offensive text message. It was so bad, her mother reported it, and we traced it. To your phone, Jonathan."

I opened my mouth, and then I closed it again. I shook my head. I stamped my two feet in frustration.

"Can you explain that, Jonathan?"

"Yes," I whispered. "But you won't believe me."

"Try me."

I knew it was pointless, but I told him about the message Julie had got, and how I'd responded to it. I knew there wasn't a chance he would believe me, because I'd deleted Danielle's message off Julie's phone, in case she might see it.

"Are you sure it came from Danielle?" he said.

Of course I wasn't, not a hundred per cent. I knew it, but I couldn't swear to it. I hadn't checked. I'd deleted the filthy message almost automatically.

I shook my head.

"Well, Jonathan," he said heavily. "I might be prepared to believe your story, but it still doesn't excuse what you did. You are old enough to know that you can't go sending threatening messages like that, even if you are sure you are sending it to a person who—"

"Deserves it," I finished.

"Well . . . Look, the point is, Jonathan, we can't trust you with a young child. We aren't sure you are in control of yourself. You may be violent. You can see that we can't take that risk."

"I am *not* violent!" I screamed.

Kate said, "Would you ever get a grip, Guard? He can't live with his sister because he is too young to look after her."

"That is true, Miss Knight, and he comes from . . . well, very difficult circumstances. He's bound to be troubled."

Kate shook her head. "That's not the point," she said.

"Troubled!" I shouted. "Yes, I am bloody troubled. I'm troubled that you won't let me see Julie."

"You can see her."

"Yeah, I can spend a few hours with her, with someone watching us all the time. That's like being on reality TV. I can't live my life like that, being watched. It's not natural."

He shrugged.

"I suppose you're going to tell me now that you found her hair in my bed," I said sarcastically. "Or my hair in hers."

"No," he said, surprised. "Should we . . . ?"

I wouldn't answer. Stupid bastards.

"Jonathan, are you trying to tell me something?" he asked.

"No, I'm bloody *not*!" I said forcefully. "I'm just saying, I know how your filthy sewer of a mind works. You think you know it all. Child abuse – it's all the rage these days. Well, listen to me, I'm not an abused child, and neither is Julie, so you can stuff your friggin' theories, right?"

Paudge said, "Julie has been abused, Jonathan. You only have to look at her face. Poor little scrap."

I wasn't going to buy that. He needn't think he was going to get around me that way.

"You know that was only a once-off," I said. "I told you the whole story."

"And the whole story is one of abuse and neglect, Jonathan, and whatever way you look at it, these things go down the generations, you know."

Well, I'd got it out of him, his creepy suspicions, but there was no satisfaction in it. I don't know why I'd even persisted.

That thing about the generations, it made me think of Granda and his mad notions. He was Da's da. But Da was totally different. I think. And as for Gramma. There's no one else like her in the family. Not a single one.

"You could have counselling," he added.

"Counselling!" I spat the word. "I don't need fucking counselling. I need to be with Julie."

"No can do, son," he said.

"You can see Jonathan every week," they promised Julie after the funeral.

"And we can talk on the phone," I said, trying to make it easier for her. "Have you got a charger?" I asked Jean. "She'll need to charge her phone up."

Jean looked at Kate. I swear she was wondering whether it was all right for Julie and me to ring each other. Christ almighty, what sort of a hellhole have I fallen into?

Kate – God bless her pretty amethyst ring – ignored Jean's look and answered my question for her. "Of course Jean will have a charger, Jonathan. Is it a Nokia? If there is no charger in Jean's house, we'll get one."

"And Kate will bring Jonathan to your house to visit," they said.

"Where's my house?" Julie asked in this pathetic little voice.

"Jean's house is your house now," they said.

"I want to go home!" she wailed. "I want to go home!"

"You're cruel!" I shouted at them. "Listen to her! You're worse than Ma was. All Ma ever did was thwack her one. She'll get over that, but she'll never get over this."

But they just patted me on the arm, on the back, on the shoulder. They didn't answer.

Julie was still wailing those words as they dragged her off and shoved her into a car.

I want to go home!

I hear it in my sleep, that wretched, uncomprehending cry. It curdles the very pathways of my blood; it stops up the chambers of my heart.

chapter sixteen

When I got home from the funeral I went to check on my blade.

I'd

KILLED

my mother – I hadn't, but I had – and I'd lost my little sister.

It was none of my fault and it was all my fault.

My

HEART was broken.

and I couldn't see any way to repair it.

And you can't really go on living with a great big gash in your HEART, can you?

It's like every breath hurts, and it's all too exhausting.

I picked up the blade and I slashed my wrist.

Not deep.
Not into the vein,
just scored the skin.
It still hurt like hell.

I was just checking that the blade was sharp enough.

chapter seventeen

In the morning, I snuck into the sitting room and I got the blade again, and I held it to the skin of my wrist. I could feel my heart thumping. But then my stomach rumbled, so I went down to breakfast first.

You would not believe how much blood there is in your arm. I suppose the arm empties out first and then the blood that is in the rest of you sort of comes pumping in to fill up the empty veins and then it all comes out too. Gallons of it. Red liquid everywhere, all over your clothes and your sheets and the floor and everything. Stinking hot.

That's how I imagined it anyway. I read about it on the computer, and that's how I imagined it would look.

The staff would be furious. Not the cleaners, though they would not actually be all that very delighted either, I suppose. But I mean the care staff. The ones who are supposed to be keeping us alive so that blokes like Paudge Rooney can go on thinking up awful crimes we might have committed to torture us with.

Most days I just stayed in bed. They didn't like that. They came and tried to haul me out. They said I had to go to school.

I had to get dressed. I had to get washed. I had to eat. I don't see why, I said, but they clucked and they argued and in the end I would say, Come back in an hour, and I will get up then. But I wouldn't. They said they'd have to get a doctor for me. I said, Yeah, yeah, cool. That calmed them down for a while. They mean well, but they'd drive you to drink. Or to suicide. Nice to know I have that blade, just in case.

They set me up with this school. It's not really school, it's more a kind of training course. I wouldn't go, though. I couldn't bear to get out of bed, much less go and face a classroom full of people I don't know.

In the afternoons, if Kate came, I would get up for a while and sit in my dressing gown to talk to her.

She came to see me most days, and once a week she took me to see Julie. For the longest time, I couldn't work out whether it was more painful to see her or not to see her, but Kate kept saying that Julie needed me.

I wasn't sure if she really thought that or if she was just saying it to make me feel better. But I got up on the Julie days.

chapter eighteen

They found the goddamn blade in the sitting room one day, and there was blue murder, as Gramma used to say. I hadn't thought about her for days, and then I suddenly missed her like mad, like an ache in my guts.

They lined us all up and shouted at us. You couldn't blame them, I suppose. Their jobs were on the line. Suppose some inspector-type person had found the blade? They'd all be sacked, I'd say. I wouldn't much care, I don't exactly like any of them, but I suppose I might feel a bit guilty. Maybe they have little kids and need the money, you know?

They said nobody was going to leave the room until they found out about the blade, and the other lads were furious because it was swimming that day and they were going to miss the bus, so I owned up, and they sent me to my room and got the doctor. The bleedin' doctor! You have to laugh. What is the doctor going to do about it? But they don't know what else to do, so they call the doctor. I suppose she is a head doctor. I wouldn't talk to her.

So then bloody Kate came, and she read me the riot act. They'd put the blade on a saucer, like it was

Exhibit A, and they actually brought it into the room to show Kate. As if she needed to see what a blade looked like.

You could see she thought this was a tad over the top. She put the saucer on the windowsill, out of the way, so she wouldn't have to keep seeing it on the coffee table while she was talking to me.

"Jonathan," she said, "I am not going to ask you what the blade is about. I think we both know what it's about?"

She is dead clever like that. Anyone else would have started into me, shouting and screaming about why did I have the blade and I would start having to think up ridiculous reasons.

I shrugged.

"So we're on the same hymn sheet, are we?"

"What? What hymn sheet?"

"Page, then, Jonathan. We're on the same page, are we?"

"Yeah," I said. "I suppose."

"OK, then. So if you are thinking like that, you need to stop thinking like that, Jonathan. And think about *Julie*."

"I *am* thinking about Julie," I roared. "It's because I can't bloody stop thinking about Julie . . ."

"Rubbish," she said grimly. "It's not Julie you're thinking about at all. It's yourself."

"How do you make that out?" I snuffled into my sleeve.

I thought, The one person in the world I might get a bit of sympathy from, and here she was giving me a hard time.

"What?" she said.

"I *said*," I said, "how do you make that out? That I am not thinking about Julie."

"Because I am enormously clever and I know and understand everything," she said sourly.

I knew that meant *Because it is as plain as the nose on your face.*

"How could you be so *sel—*?"

She stopped herself from saying it, but I heard it all the same.

"I'm *not*," I hissed.

"Sorry," she mumbled. "I know that, Jono. Sorry. OK, tell

me about it. Explain it to me."

"I am just nothing but trouble," I said. "Julie would be better off."

I don't know what made me say that. It's what suicidey people say on the TV, I suppose. I thought it was as good a line as any, but you can't fool Kate.

Kate shook her head and sighed and ran her fingers through her hair. Then she put a hand on my arm and she shook it a little bit, as if to try to get through to me.

"Listen," she said. "You are all that little girl has. The only family in the world. Don't—"

She could see I was going to point out that there was Da.

"He doesn't count," she said before I could bring his name up, "because he doesn't care. What about you?"

"What about me? Do I care about Julie? Of course I care about her."

"Well, you have a funny way of showing it. Would you get a grip, Signor Antonio, and stop moping about and start thinking what you can do for that little girl? She needs you. You know she does. You keep saying it. Aren't you being inconsistent?"

"But they won't let me look after her, so what's the point?"

"The point is that she needs you – not to look after her. There are adults who can do that. She needs you to be her bloody *brother*, Jonathan. That's what she needs. Her *alive* brother."

I stopped snivelling, and I looked at her.

"You're thinking about how much you want to see her. Start thinking about how much *she* wants to see *you*, and just bring a modicum of logic into it, Jonathan."

A modicum, if you don't mind. Whatever that is.

"What do you mean?"

"I mean that . . . if you are alive, you can see her. If you are dead, she will never see you again. Gettit?"

"Yeah," I muttered.

"So button up your overcoat, sunshine," she said.

"*What*?"

She really does talk in riddles, that one.

"It's a song. It means, you need to keep well and healthy for the sake of the people who love you. Get it?"

"Sing it," I said. "Go on. Sing it."

She laughed. And she did. It was a really stupid song, but the tune was great. It made me smile.

"She's only a little girl," Kate said. "Just remember that, big boy."

"How come it's always down to me?" I said. "It's not *bloody* fair."

I was waiting for that line, you know the one, *Life isn't fair, Jonathan.* But she didn't say that. That is the single best thing about Kate. She never says, *Life isn't fair, Jonathan.* I hate people who say that, as if they have this great insight into how the world ticks and they need to share it with you. Bloody smug bastards they are.

What she said was, "It's not because you're special, Jonathan. It's not even because you're you. It's because you're the only one, Jonathan. That's why it's all down to you. You have no choice. You are the only thing she's got."

Great, I thought. Bleedin' marvellous. It all depends on me. I'm like the fella in the story that's holding up the earth. He's thrown forward on to his knees, and he's got the world on his back. Poor eejit. Hercules. No, Atlas.

I said that to Kate, about Atlas, and she said, Well, maybe it feels like the whole world, but it's not, you know. It's only Julie, and she's not heavy.

She ain't heavy, she's my sister. Yeah, yeah, very amusing.

She took the blade with her when she left.

chapter nineteen

They'd decided not to press charges, Kate told me one day.

"Really?" I said. "That's nice of them."

"Sarky. Good sign," said Kate comfortably.

You can't win with her. She's always a step ahead of you. But I might as well go on being sarky, I thought, since it made her feel so positive.

"Would that mean that they are not going to charge me with killing my mother, or beating up Julie, or holding up the petrol station, or sending the threatening text message, or are there some other crimes they've invented not to charge me with?"

"All of the above," she said.

We sat there for a while, not speaking. Then I sighed and I looked up at her and said, "Well then." Meaning, more or less, *So that's that, then*.

She nodded, and then she said, "The quality of mercy is not strained, Jonathan. It droppeth as the gentle rain from heaven upon the place beneath. It is twice blest: it blesseth him that gives and him that takes."

I stared at her.

"Jeez, you've lost it, Kato," I said. "You've really gone and lost it now. What are we going to tell your mother?"

She laughed.

"It just came into my head," she said, "when I was telling you that they are not going to prosecute you. It's from *The Merchant of Venice*. Remember?"

How could I forget? I still had the copy belonging to Mr O'Connell that Julie had brought for me from home.

"You're smiling," she said. "So maybe you won't kill yourself today?"

This was a joke she had, that every time she made me laugh, I was one step further away from suicide. Some people call that black humour, but it suits me.

"Not today," I said.

"Remember when you thought I was going to try to save you with Shakespeare?"

I smiled. "That was a stupid idea."

"Yes," she said. "But it wasn't an idea I ever had."

"Say it again," I said.

"Sam," she added.

"Yeah, Sam. Say it again, Sam. I liked it."

So she repeated it, about the quality of mercy. I didn't understand it all, but I liked the sound of it.

"So basically it means it's great stuff altogether, this mercy," I said. "Double portions all round."

"You've got it," she said.

"Are you trying to tell me they are being merciful?" I asked then. "Like, they're being nice to me, not pressing charges?"

"No," she said. "I'm not trying to tell you anything. I just remembered the quotation."

"It blesseth . . ." I said.

"Him that gives and him that takes," she finished. "Yeah, that's why it's twice blessed, see?"

"And I am him that takes?" I said. I was starting to feel the smallest bit uncomfortable about this.

"No. Not necessarily," she said.

"I could be the one that *gives*?" I said, puzzled.

She shrugged.

"You're a smart one," she said. "You should go to school. It'd do you a power of good."

After she left, I went and got the book and opened it at random, to see if I could find the speech about mercy, but instead I noticed where it said "Dermot O'Connell, Second Year" on the first page, in faded ink. It must have been his copy from school. I didn't know his name was Dermot.

I found this line I liked, and I wrote it out on a piece of paper and left it propped on my table, so I could show it to Kate next time. We have to have something to talk about, and I don't always want it to be me.

She laughed when she saw it: "Love me, and leave me not."

I was shocked that she laughed. I thought she would start banging on again about Julie and I would be able to say, "Yes, I understand now," but instead she just gave this throaty gurgle and shook her head in amusement.

"What's so funny?" I said. "It's like a line from a song, isn't it? Like Bob Dylan or some kinda crap like that, isn't it?"

"Wash your mouth out," she said. "Bob Dylan isn't crap. You're just too young to appreciate him."

That wasn't what I'd meant, but I didn't argue about it. I just waved the quotation at her, and I said, "So why is it funny?"

"Well, put it like this, Shakespeare thought it was a terrible line."

"He wrote it," I said.

"Maybe, but as a kind of joke."

"Well, it's in his play," I said. "Anyway, I don't care what feckin' Shakespeare thought about it. I like it."

"Good for you," she said. "You're entitled."

"Gee, thanks," I said.

Later I said, "I've been thinking about this youth course thing."

"Oh yes?" she said, looking interested. The social worker in her was popping up in her eyes.

"I don't want to go on it," I said.

"Oh!" She looked crestfallen, though I could see she was trying not to. "Ah, well."

"No, because, see, why would I want to go to a place like that, when I have a perfectly good school already, with a Mr O'Connell in it?"

And one or two other people.

"Who's . . . oh, the one who gave you the book?"

"Yeah. His own copy, from when he was at school." I showed her the autograph on the front page.

"That was nice of him," she agreed.

Bloody nice, I thought.

"Well, we could see if there's a bus from here that would take you near your old school. Will I see if I can find out?"

I shrank back a bit. I'd only just been thinking about it. I didn't like being rushed.

She looked at me. "I could leave it till next week, if you like," she said.

"Yeah, that'd be better. Cool. Thanks."

After she'd left, I sat for a while with the book on my knee, thinking about everything that had gone on and thinking mostly about Julie, and all the time "Love me, and leave me not" was gliding in and out of my mind, like a kind of music.

I hadn't rung Annie. I'd promised her at the church, and I hadn't done it. She'd sent me a few texts. Just cheerful nothings. I couldn't respond. I couldn't find my cheerful self.

I still couldn't ring her, but I texted her the line. *Love me, and leave me not.* I added in the scene and line number from *The Merchant* (that's what the cool people call it, the actors, Kate told me; she acts, wouldn't you know it?) so she wouldn't think . . . well, I knew she'd know what I meant. Annie is sound. I'll see her soon.

And then I went and asked them for a postcard, and I wrote a note to Julie. I could have sent her a text, but they check all her texts, and I don't like the idea of them reading it, even though there is nothing secret that I have to say to her. A postcard is open anyway, and I don't mind if they read it.

This is what I wrote:

Dear Julie

Hope you're OK. I'm going
back to school next week.
See you on Tuesday as usual.
Love you to bits. Jonathan

Then I added a P.S.:

We can play Happy Families
if you like

And all along the bottom I put a row of kisses, like tiny stitches.

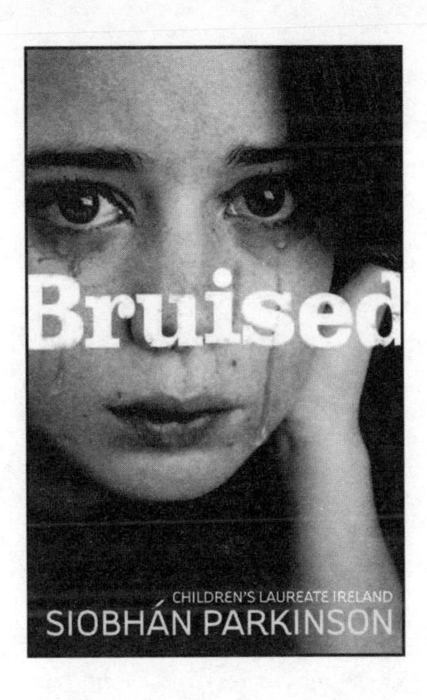

The idea for BRUISED began to form in Siobhán Parkinson's mind when she heard a woman on the radio telling the story of her childhood with an alcoholic mother. One day, when there was no food in the house, the mother had come home with a bag of apples for the children's dinner. "What struck me," says Parkinson, "was how that one incident had such a hold on the adult who had been that child. Many things had happened in that house that were much more shocking than being given only apples for your dinner, but somehow those apples had become a metaphor for all the abuse and neglect she had suffered in childhood. I mulled over that image of the apples for years, and then one day, I remembered a question a little girl had asked me once at a reading in Dublin: 'Would you ever think of writing a book where the mammy dies?'That sad little question, which went to my heart at the time, began to rattle around in my head along with the apples, and a few lines that my nephew had been quoting from T*he Merchant of Venice*, which he was reading at school – and suddenly it all fell into place, and I began to write a story about a brother and sister, Jono and Julie, who live with an alcoholic mother, in a home where the love has gone bad."